The Ties That Bind

Florida Sheriff Deputies Murder Mysteries

ABSOLUTELY AMAZING eBOOKS

Habent Sua Fata Libelli

ABSOLUTELY AMAZING eBOOKS

Manhanset House
Shelter Island Hts., New York 11965-0342

bricktower@aol.com • tech@absolutelyamazingebooks.com
• absolutelyamazingebooks.com

Library of Congress Cataloging-in-Publication Data
Jarvis, Angela
The ties that bind
p. cm.
      1. FICTION / Thrillers / Suspense. 2. FICTION / Thrillers / Crime.
        3. FICTION / Mystery & Detective / Hard-Boiled.
          Fiction, I. Title.
      ISBN: 978-1-9511501-2-9, Trade Paper

August 2022

The Ties That Bind

Florida Sheriff Deputies
Murder Mysteries

Book 3

Angela Jarvis

For everyone who keeps buying my books
and encouraging me to write the next one.
Thank you.

Books in the
Florida Sheriff Deputies
Murder Mysteries series

Wages of Sin

Secrets We Keep

The Ties That Bind

AbsolutelyAmazingEbooks.com

Table of Contents

"Truth will ultimately prevail,
when there is pains to bring it to light."
- George Washington

Prologue

Tony Giovanni shook his head to help clear his mind. He had been daydreaming again about cerulean waters, palm trees, and a red head with a fiery attitude. He had just returned from working a case in the Florida Keys, where he had met her. She was the sister of the detective he had worked with down there, and he couldn't seem to get her out of his head.

Enough of that, he thought shaking his head to clear it. He had another job to do. When reading the newspaper earlier in the week, a familiar name had popped out at him. It was the name of his college roommate, Dagan Murphy. It seemed after ten years of Dagan's sister being missing, they had finally found her remains, and had laid her to rest. She was the reason they had met. Dagan had decided to go into law enforcement because of his sister's disappearance, and the two guys had shared a room in a dorm at FSU.

Call it fate, coincidence, or whatever else it could be chalked up to, he had been planning to call his old buddy in relation to some cold cases he had been studying, and then out of the blue, his name appeared in the Tallahassee Daily Journal.

He felt the case from the Florida Keys had some definite tie-ins with some cold cases in the Northwest Florida area, and he intended to head that way soon. He knew that he would need the cooperation of the law enforcement agencies in the area, and usually that wasn't a big deal with cold cases.

He was going to call Dagan and ask him if he could depend on his help, both as a professional, and as a friend. Picking up the phone to dial the number he had found through law enforcement resources, he smiled, eager to talk to his old buddy.

He had no way of knowing the Pandora's box that was about to be opened, or the profound effect it would have on them both.

Chapter One

Tony followed the directions that he had programmed into the GPS in his SUV. Never having been in this part of Florida, he found it quite a daunting task finding his way around. One could easily get lost in the wilderness landscape that was unlike no other part of the sunshine state.

It was heavily wooded country with forest on both sides of the state road he was currently on. There were very few signs to go by, but there were plenty of dirt roads you could turn onto from the main highway.

No thanks, he thought. Those roads could lead to just about anywhere. There were probably shotguns and banjos at the end of a few of them.

He was a city boy, so this was certainly going to be an adventure. It wasn't something he would willingly sign up for, but he had a job to do, and he took it seriously.

He was careful to keep an eye on the GPS for the exact location of the turn off to the road that would lead him to Dagan's house. They had both been criminal justice majors at FSU and had kept in touch for several years after graduation but had lost contact in recent years.

Tony had applied to the FBI academy after college graduation, and Dagan had returned to his home town and was working for the county sheriff's department. He had recently been appointed acting sheriff until one could be elected. It seemed the sheriff that Dagan worked for had died under some rather strange circumstances recently. Dagan had promised to tell him all about it over a few cold ones.

According to the GPS, the turnoff he was anticipating was in five hundred feet. Slowing down, Tony could see it was a dirt road that had recently been graded. He took the turn carefully.

It looked like something you would see in an antique store oil painting. The early morning sunlight filtered through the trees in spots giving it a very ethereal glow. The tops of the trees on both sides of the road had grown overhead, forming an arch over the red dirt road. The leaves on the trees had dew clinging to them and would sparkle every now and then. This isn't so bad, he thought.

Up ahead he spotted a small doe off to one side of the road. He slowed again, having been warned by Dagan, that they had a tendency to jump in front of moving vehicles causing accidents. It stared at him briefly, then bounded off, disappearing into the brush.

Driving in this peaceful place gave him time to reflect on the case he had just been part of in the Florida Keys. Several young women had turned up dead, and some of the details of the case had caused a flag to come up on some cold cases he had in a database.

Once he arrived in the Keys and had a chance to talk to the lead detective Valerie Mason, he quickly learned her suspicions were headed in the right direction, but she had mistakenly suspected the wrong person.

Tony, along with another undercover agent that was posing as an assistant pastor at a local church, were there to keep an eye on the suspect, who happened to be the real pastor of the church they had under surveillance. Turned out the good reverend had murdered several women because of their chosen lifestyles. He decided their sins needed to be punished, and in doing so he could save their souls. He had even killed his own daughter years ago, who had become pregnant at sixteen, and the father of the baby. The man had been the definition of pure evil.

As he drove along this scenic route, it was hard to believe that kind of evil could exist in a place such as this. Sadly, he knew that the most beautiful of places could harbor the ugliest of sins.

He had never given a thought to living in the country, but this place seemed peaceful, and so far away from what he was used to, it would sure make a convincing argument.

Before he realized it, the winding driveway Dagan had described to him appeared on his right. He turned in and drove a short distance before the road opened up into a beautiful yard with an old-style Florida cracker house sitting dead center with a wide wrap around porch.

Dagan's patrol vehicle was parked to one side. He couldn't help but smile. It would be good to see his old friend after all these years, and even better for the chance to work with him.

He honked the horn to alert Dagan to his presence and shut the engine off. He sat there a moment to see if anyone would come to the door. The only sound in this quiet little corner of the country was the engine of his SUV making popping and pinging noises as it cooled.

Suddenly Dagan appeared from around the side of the house on the porch flanked on either side by two huge dogs. He hadn't changed a bit. He couldn't help but grin from ear to ear and saw Dagan doing the same.

Tony opened the door and hopped out to greet his old friend.

Chapter Two

A few hours together, and after a few beers had been consumed, it was as if the years between the old friends had melted away.

They talked about everything from their careers and love lives, to the incidents that had led them to being here in the same place once again.

Tony sat in amazement as Dagan had explained that his old high school rival Wade and co-worker at the sheriff's department, had turned out to be his half-brother. The sheriff, Alice Taylor that Dagan had replaced, had an affair with Dagan's father and Wade had been the result of that affair. Through extenuating circumstances, after Wade was given up for adoption, his adoptive parents had him admitted to the Oakville Children's Asylum where he had endured some awful things.

Once Wade found out the truth of his birth, one day after school he had met with Rachel, Dagan's sixteen-year-old sister to tell her the truth. Wade told her who he was and of course she accused him of lying. Knowing that she needed to find out for sure if Wade was telling her the truth or not, she went to confront Alice, her godmother, hoping to find out Wade was nothing but a liar. When Alice reluctantly confirmed what Wade had said she tried explaining things to Rachel. There was a confrontation when Rachel tried to attack Alice and Rachel fell hitting her head, causing her death. Alice, the newly elected sheriff, covered it up to protect her secret and her career.

"Man, that had to be hard to find out after all these years." Tony said incredulously. "How's your mom taking it?"

"About as good as any woman who finds out her husband had an affair that produced an illegitimate child with her best friend, who it also turns out is responsible for the death of her only daughter and then covered it up for ten years."

"It sounds like a movie plot, not real at all."

"Oh, it's real. We are starting to recover, especially since we found my sister's remains and finally laid her to rest. My family has always been strong, we'll make it."

"No doubt man."

There was an awkward silence for a couple of minutes then Dagan broke it by asking, "Want to go get some Mexican food for dinner? There's a great restaurant in town."

"Sounds good to me. Mind if I shower before we go, it was a long drive?"

"Go ahead. The bathroom is down the hall, last door on your right. The guest room is the door right before the bathroom"

Tony retreated down the hall and Dagan took his twin golden retrievers, Kojak and Columbo, out for exercise and a bathroom break.

Tony had told Dagan a little about the case he had worked in the Florida Keys and how that case had brought him here, but he hadn't given all the details. Dagan found it such a coincidence that Tony's case could be tied to some all the way up here in the panhandle. If there was one thing that Dagan had learned in life, nothing was ever as it seemed, and you never really knew anybody, not even those who were closest to you.

Alice and Wade, as well as his own father, had taught him that.

~ ~ ~

Over the best steak fajitas this side of the Mexican border, Tony had at last given Dagan all the details he had left out earlier.

It seemed there had been a preacher that had committed murders over a span of at least twenty years that they knew of, possibly more, and he was here to find out just how many more could be tied to him. He had been tracked down to the Keys where he was preaching at a church on the island of Big Pine Key. After two bodies were found and the investigation heated up, the so-called man of God kidnapped a Monroe County deputy and intended the same fate for her as he had for his other victims. She had simply gotten in his way. When he was attempting to escape the authorities, he shot her, but she survived. He was not as fortunate.

Another officer, Detective Morris, had ended the preacher's life by putting a bullet in him, stopping the preacher's predilection of killing women he thought needed to be saved from their sinful lives. The sad part of it all was the detective had been good friends with the preacher, so it had been rough on the old guy. He retired soon after.

"I know the feeling of seeing someone you thought you knew turn into a stranger. It's very unsettling and can leave you questioning everything. It makes you wonder who you can trust." Dagan said stoically.

"I have a couple boxes of records on the *good* reverend. I am hoping you can help me sort through it all. When I did a record search on his driver's license, I found his first one was issued right here in Washington County. I guess he lived here as a young man before moving to Tallahassee.

Dagan's mind starting swirling with possibilities. He had quite a few cold cases that stretched back a number of years. Could some of them possibly be connected with this Lockhart guy?

"I think we have our work cut out for us bud." Dagan told him.

"I'm sure we do. Nothing in this job ever comes easy."

The waitress came back around with their check and Tony grabbed it before Dagan could.

"Just my way of thanking you for a place to stay while we work on all of this."

"It's not necessary Tony."

"No, but I'm doing it anyway."

Chapter Three

Dagan and Tony spent the better part of Friday night digging through the boxes of records that Tony had brought with him from Tallahassee. It was in the early hours of the morning when they decided that they could do a much better job after getting some sleep.

Tony was awakened the next morning by the smell of coffee and bacon frying. His stomach began rumbling, urging him out of bed. He pulled on a pair of jeans and a t-shirt, then made his way down the hall and into the kitchen. He was shocked to see a stunning strawberry blonde sitting at the table sipping on a cup of coffee.

"Good morning. You must be Dani. I've heard so much about you that I feel as if I know you." He announced as he entered the kitchen.

"I could say the same about you." She smiled at him. She reminded him instantly of someone else. Another red head he had met in the Keys. He still hadn't decided what, if anything, he was going to do about it. That young woman had a bit of a troubled past, but her sister was a deputy, and assured him that she had straightened her life out for the better.

He reached for an empty cup sitting by the coffee pot and poured himself some black coffee. He needed to get focused on the work at hand and keep his personal life out of the way until a better time came along to deal with it.

"So, what's on the agenda for today Boss?" Dagan asked as he took an appreciative sip of coffee.

"I was thinking that if our preacher received his first license up here, he had to be a teenager. With that being said, he had to have some family around here. I think maybe we should start digging in that direction and see what we come up with."

"That shouldn't be too hard. This area has some very prominent family names that have been a part of the county history since it became a county. That, and everyone knows everyone else and their business." Dagan said with a grin

"Ahhh, the perks of small-town living. Gotta love it." Dani rolled her eyes and laughed.

Dagan brought a small platter of bacon, eggs and toast over and placed it in the center of the table. "Dig in everyone. There's plenty."

They talked a bit about the information they thought was relevant from the search last night and the ideas they had on how to use it.

"I own a bookstore that has some copies of books that might come in handy like certain family histories and maps of the county. You never know what or who might be mentioned." Dani offered.

"They might be needed. Thanks for the offer." Tony said appreciatively.

"No problem. I make a pretty good research assistant."

"She sure does. She helped point out some key names from old year books in the case we were discussing last night over supper." Dagan chimed in.

"Well, we might have to put her on the payroll, figuratively speaking." Tony chuckled.

"Oh, that's alright. I'm used to working for free for the sheriff in this town. His pay rate is about the same as yours." Dani winked at Dagan and they all chuckled.

After they finished eating, they enjoyed a second cup of coffee. Dani enjoyed listening to the two men catch up and reminisce about old times. It was mostly Tony telling her stories about Dagan from their college days, hoping to get him in trouble, but Dagan took it with good humor and pointed out that Toni had made a few wild and stupid decisions himself.

"Well boys, I hate to break up the fun, but someone has to sell books in this town. It was really nice meeting you Tony." She smiled warmly. "Please keep him out of trouble, would you?"

"I will do my best, but no promises. It was nice meeting you too."

Dagan walked Dani out to her Jeep. "You never told me your college roommate was such a hottie." She teased, poking him in the chest with her finger.

"A hottie? Umm, I have never considered Tony Giovanni a hottie, nor will I ever." He tried to keep a serious face. "Why haven't you ever called me a hottie?" he asked raising an eyebrow.

"I have told lots of people you're a hottie, just not to your face." She grabbed his chin and gave it a little pinch. "I wouldn't want you to get the big head or anything."

"Oh, ok. As long as I don't have to worry about you and Casanova in there."

She slapped him playfully on the shoulder. "Of course not. But it doesn't hurt to keep you on your toes."

"I'll remember that the next time we are at the beach and a pretty girl in a bikini walks by."

"That's different. He's not in there half naked."

"I was his roommate and I've seen him half naked. There is nothing pretty about it, trust me."

"You wouldn't know a good-looking man if you saw one."

"Sure, I would. I see one every day when I look in the mirror." He said with a devilish grin.

"Oh, let me just hop up in my jeep, it's getting deep out here." She said sarcastically and gave him a light peck on the lips.

He held the door open for her and then closed it after she got seated. Leaning through the window he told her he would call when he got a chance. He wasn't sure where today's investigation would lead them. After another brief kiss, she left for town.

Dagan walked back in the house to find Tony already going over the files they had left scattered on the coffee table the night before.

"Let me just clean up and I'll be back to help." Dagan said.

"No need, I put everything in the dishwasher and wiped the table down."

"Thanks, but that wasn't necessary."

"No problem. I just thought I'd do it, so we could get started when you came back in. You were out there long enough that I just happened to finish" Tony teased.

"I was defending myself."

"Oh really. What did you do wrong? Or was it something I said that got you in trouble?" Tony was laughing, enjoying the thought of Dagan getting in trouble for something he had told Dani earlier.

"No, I didn't get in trouble. Dani thinks you're a *hottie*. Whatever the hell that means." Dagan sounded miffed.

Now Tony was belly laughing. "Oh, your girl likes me better. Just like old times."

"She does not like you better. She wanted to know why I never told her you were good looking."

"Why didn't you?"

"Because I don't think you are! As a matter of fact, I always thought those dark brooding eyes and that little cleft in your chin that reminds people of Clint Eastwood makes you ugly." Now they were both laughing.

Tony grabbed his side. "Ok, stop. I haven't laughed this hard in a long time, and apparently those muscles are letting me know."

They both settled down and took seats opposite the other at the dining room table. They each made notes on things that they thought important and needed further research. Dagan was going to get Tony set up at an empty desk with a computer at the office to give him better access to all records and resources online for the county on Monday morning. He was more than willing to help his old pal, but he still had a county to run also. It would be much easier to work with Tony if they shared office space and Tony wasn't stuck out here in the woods, while Dagan was in town at the office, not to mention, Tony didn't know his way around.

Neither man could know, as they sat going through the records that revealed partial truths about the preacher, that their case would soon take a turn that neither would ever see coming.

Chapter Four

Dagan was reading Donald Lockhart's birth certificate. It was just your average run of the mill birth record. There were no clues he could discern other than the names of his parents. The name Lockhart didn't sound even remotely familiar to him. He had lived here his entire life and could not recall anyone with that last name. Of course, there were the surrounding counties people travelled back and forth between, and people had relatives in most of them. The counties of the panhandle were all closely knit together. That should narrow it down, he thought sarcastically.

He made a mental note to ask around and see if anyone knew of this family. He would be certain to ask him mom and get Dani to look up the family land records for the county. The preacher's mother had been a Donovan before marrying his father. He would check into that name as well. He looked up and out the huge window that looked over the station and could see Tony working at the desk he had set up for him. He seemed very intent on whatever it was he was reading.

Dagan got up from his desk to stretch his back and legs and walked out of his office to see what Tony was up to. As he approached him, he asked, "What do you have there that's so intense?"

"Well, we knew about the speeding tickets that the old reverend had but look what I managed to dig up. It was buried in juvie records but was never sealed. It seems that as a young teen, he had a penchant for spying on girls through their bedroom windows. According to the report, he was released to the custody of David Lockhart. Maybe he was his grandfather or an uncle or something."

"Have you run his name?"

"Just about to." With a few strokes on the keyboard, they found out that David Lockhart was indeed the brother to Dale Lockhart, making him Donald's uncle. "I wonder why his uncle picked him up and not his parents."

"Who knows. Now at least we have a starting point with relatives."

"Does it say if there was any type of punishment, community service or such?"

"It doesn't look like there's any mention of it here. I'll keep digging through everything and we might get lucky."

"Ok. I have to go out on a call. One of my deputies answered a call to some stolen cattle, but the rancher demanded to speak to the sheriff and that would be me." he said exasperated. "I've been putting it off all morning, but I need to get out there and get it taken care of."

"That's what happens when you're the big guy in charge." Tony smirked at him.

"You just remember that, who's in charge and all."

"If I forget, I'll just ask Dani." Tony knew that would get to him.

Dagan just pointed his finger at him as if to say you better watch yourself, and then walked away. He could hear Tony chuckling behind his back. It was good to have his old friend around again. They always got along well, and now having the chance to work together was something else. Although Tony

18

had far more education, Dagan had the street experience. It seemed that they were going to make a good team.

When Dagan was through dealing with his local call, he was going to talk to his mom and see if there were any people she could recall by the last name Lockhart. If anybody knew, she might. She had worked for the department of Children and Families for years as a counselor before her retirement. She had only got to spend seven months of that retirement with his dad before he had passed away. She could've returned to work but chose to stay home, and work on writing the book she had wanted to write since she was a young girl and dreamed of becoming a bestselling author. She had mentioned that she had begun working on it not long ago. Dagan couldn't swear to it, but he thought she might be using the experience with Alice as part of the story. If so, his mom had a huge part in it, so it was her story to tell. Dani had promised a huge book launch and signing at the bookstore, when it went to publication, and he would be there cheering her on, always the proud son. His mama needed something good in her life.

~ ~ ~

Dagan heard his cell phone ringing. He had left it sitting in the console of his patrol truck, with the window down so he could hear it. It gave him the perfect excuse to break away from the conversation that the old farmer whose cattle had been stolen had engaged him for the last half hour.

Walking over he grabbed up the phone and answered it but not soon enough. It was dead on the other end. He could see it had been Tony that had called, and he got an alert that said he had left a message. He told the farmer that he had a work-related call and would have to say goodbye but would have his ag department working on it and would get back to him as soon as he had any information.

He listened to Tony's message as soon as he cranked the truck.

"Dagan, you are never going to believe what I just uncovered. Our two cases are more connected than we ever could have thought. See you soon. Bye"

Nothing like leaving somebody hanging, Dagan thought. He put the truck in gear and headed back towards the office. On the way he couldn't help but wonder what could be so interesting that Tony would call and leave a message. Other than the fact that the preacher turned out to be a serial killer and Dagan had plenty of cases in this area of missing people that could be some of his victims, he didn't really see how there could be any other connections. He had never even heard of the guy or his family. His questions would soon be answered as he pulled into the station parking lot.

Walking through the door to the office he could see Tony pacing back and forth by his desk and holding a stack of papers flipping through them furiously. When he saw Dagan, he made a beeline straight for him. He was shaking the small stack of papers in his hand. Dagan wanted to laugh, but he could read the seriousness on Tony's face. There was an odd excitement too.

"I was looking through records pertaining to the preacher's parents. Quite a few documents come up such as land patents and tax records. The most interesting thing that came up was the fact that his father had a daughter from a previous marriage. The preacher had an older sister. If we can find her and talk to her, we may get some insight on all of this which will make it easier to solve some of these cases." He spoke hopefully.

"What's her name?" Dagan now shared in Tony's excitement.

"Andrea Lockhart. She would be fifty-eight years old. We just have to track her down."

"That's great. Hopefully she is still around here. Like I said that name is not familiar at all."

"It's a start. I've got a scan running now to find her name in several different databases."

"Let me know what comes up. I'm going to write up a report on the case from this morning while it's fresh in my mind."

Dagan headed to his office and removed his hat, hanging it on the coatrack near the door. He took a seat and decided to call his mother before doing the report now that he had another family members name of the Lockhart family to work with. The phone rang several times before he heard his mom's soft southern accent say hello.

"Hey mama."

"Hey there son. Good to hear from you. I haven't seen you in over two weeks." She chastised gently.

"I know mama. I'm sorry, I've just been busy preparing for Tony's arrival. He got in Friday night. I'm planning on bringing him over one night. I know you haven't seen each other since graduation."

"It'll be lovely to see him again. Let me know when y'all are coming out and I'll cook some lasagna." His mom knew that lasagna had been his favorite meal since he was a little boy.

"Sounds great. Not to change the subject, but I have a question for you."

"What is it?"

"Did you ever hear of any families around this area with the last name of Lockhart?"

"That name sure doesn't ring any bells. I might have heard it over the years at one time or another, but if I did, it must not have left any kind of impression."

"It's a name that's attached to something I'm working on and Tony and I are trying to find any living relatives of the person that we're investigating and that is his family name. We have some proof that he lived in this area when he was a teen, so we figured he had to have relatives of some kind around here. We know he had a sister named Andrea, but we haven't found anything on her yet either. I thought you might know the name because they would have been around yours and dads age."

"Sorry son. Nothing comes to mind. If anything does, I'll let you know. If I knew where my old yearbooks were packed away, I would look through them to see if I could find him or his sister. I learned that trick from a very smart deputy I know." She teased causing Dagan to smile.

"Thanks mom. I'll let you know about the lasagna." He said his goodbyes and hung up the phone. He looked up and out the window over the office floor and Tony caught his attention and waved at him. Dagan walked over to Tony's desk.

"I managed to track down Andrea Lockhart's birth certificate. Her mother's name was Celeste Miller. It looks like she died from tuberculosis when Andrea was about a year and a half old. I guess the father remarried and had Donald with the second wife in 1963."

"Interesting. I asked my mom and she didn't recall anyone by that name, but she said she would let us know if she thought of anything. Do you want to take a break and grab lunch?"

"I'm not hungry. I'll keep digging here and see what else turns up. When I get on a roll, I don't take breaks for anything."

"You're going to work yourself into an early grave man."

"I'll be alright. This is just how I work."

"How about I bring you something back?"

"Sure, if it'll make you feel better *mom*." He muttered.

Dagan grinned and shook his head. He remembered in college when they were studying for finals, Tony was the same way. Some things never changed he guessed.

He walked back to his office and grabbed his hat from the coat rack by the door and told the receptionist where he was headed.

He was going to get a huge Italian sub, and then cross the street to see the love of his life. Dani had told him she had books written by local historians that had different maps of plots of lands owned by the more prominent family names in the area. Hopefully, this family had been well off enough to own some land.

It was a long shot, but one worth taking.

Chapter Five

The Oakville Children's Asylum had stood looming forebodingly in the woods just outside the town of Chipley for many years. It had been the focus of an investigation a few months back when the skeletal remains of a young woman had been found by two teen boys searching for ghosts. Dagan had thought they might be his sister's.

They weren't. Sadly, they were still lying in a box at the county morgue. Whoever she had been in life, she was still holding strong to that secret in death. That might be one mystery that would never be solved.

When Dagan woke up this morning, he never thought he would once again be called out there. He was wrong.

He told Tony when he walked in the kitchen for his morning cup of joe that they would be taking a small detour on the way to work.

When he explained where they would be going, Tony asked, "You mean, the same place where everything went down with your sheriff and half-brother last year?"

"The one and only."

"Wow. Do you know what it's about?'

"The contractors are out there doing some work and found some bones. They stopped digging and want to make sure they are not human. Given the history of the place, it seems to me like they did the right thing."

Tony just shook his head. "Man, we sure know how to pick cases. Or should I say, they sure know how to pick us."

"Amen to that. At least it's not cattle rustling." He said chuckling.

"I don't know how you stand the excitement you face some days."

"It's not easy, but not all of us have a cushy job in Tallahassee." Dagan jabbed jokingly.

They ate toast and drank coffee in silence as they both looked over different sections of the morning newspaper out of Panama City. There wasn't a lot going on, but it helped to stay in the know. They finished up about twenty minutes later and left the house. Dagan drove slowly, in no big hurry to go out to the asylum again. Something about the place gave him the heebie jeebies.

The long road that would take them straight to the entrance of the antebellum-like mansion's front doors emerged from seemingly out of nowhere. Dagan noticed that the guard shack that had been at the entrance to the fenced off area surrounding the property was no longer there. It wasn't like the guard did a very good job of keeping anyone out anyway.

Tony expressed his wonderment of the place. "I bet this was something to see in it's heyday. It's huge."

"This is the perfect example of looks can be deceiving. Some of the things that I discovered that went on out here would make even a hardened FBI agent like yourself want to cry. The kids that were sent here were treated like caged animals."

"I've heard that places like this were notorious for the way they treated patients. I never understood it though. People who need care and compassion the most, got treated the worst. It doesn't make any sense whatsoever."

Dagan pulled his truck up and parked by a line of other trucks with the emblem of the construction company on them. Green Ladder Construction.

Dagan asked around until he found the site foreman, a middle-aged guy by the name of Adam Young.

"Mr. Young, I'm Sheriff Murphy. I'm here about the phone call about some bones."

"Nice to meet you sheriff, and please call me Adam." He stuck his hand out to shake Dagan and Tony's in welcome.

"This is special agent Tony Giovanni, with the FBI."

"Wow, you guys call in the big dogs for some bones that were not even sure are human?"

Dagan and Tony smiled.

"No, he's here on another case and came along for the ride out here."

Adam grinned sheepishly. "Ok, let me show what we got."

They followed the man around the main building and into the back where the housing for the nurses and other staff was currently being bulldozed. It looked quite different than the last time Dagan was here. He had walked through the woods and past all those buildings when he had come here that night to find Dani, after she had been kidnapped by his half-brother. Most of the buildings were gone now. There was a small area that had been cordoned off with yellow tape that read *CAUTION*. Adam led them straight there and pointed to a small hollowed out piece of ground that contain a small pile of odds and ends bones.

Dagan and Tony knelt at the same time to examine the bones more closely. It only took both men a few seconds to determine that the bones were indeed human. A small human. A baby human.

Tony glanced up at Dagan and shook his head. They stood up and Dagan told Adam work would have to cease in the general area until they got the coroner out here.

"I was afraid of that. I'll radio my crew and tell them all to knock off." Adam said disappointed.

Dagan dug his cell phone pout of pocket and called Bill Walters, the county coroner. He explained what they had, and Bill told him he would be around in about twenty minutes. In the meantime, Dagan scanned the area quickly. He had heard rumors that a lot of children went missing over the years from here. He was beginning to wonder now if this would be the only bones found. Maybe it would be a good idea to get someone out here that was experienced in finding old graves just to make sure.

"What are your thoughts? I can see your wheels turning." Tony asked.

"For years, I've heard rumors about the children that went missing from this place. I'm wondering if this will be an isolated find, or if there could possibly be more?"

"You know the history better than I do man." Tony answered with a shrug of his shoulders.

"I'm just thinking that if there are more, it could really answer a lot of questions.

"It would mean shutting down this project temporarily."

"Yeah, I know. The contractors and investors who bought this place will be upset, but

something about this feels off."

"Follow your gut."

"With the resources you have, do you think you could get someone out here that has the equipment to look for graves?"

"Yeah, whatever you need. We have a whole unit that is equipped with GPR or ground penetrating radar for you non-FBI guys." Tony said with a grin.

"Thanks. We small town sheriffs don't have the money for all that high-falutin'

equipment." Dagan exaggerated his southern drawl.

"Let me go make a few phone calls and see when they can get out here."

"Thanks, I appreciate it."

Bill Walters came walking up about the time that Tony walked away. He had a small case in hand to help him with the examination.

"Good morning." Bill called out in greeting.

"Hey Bill. Thanks for coming out."

"Well, it is my job. Just be thankful I had finished my coffee and breakfast over at the Coffee Bean. You might've had to wait a little longer. As I like to say, the dead aren't in a hurry, so why should I be?" He said with a sardonic smile. Dagan couldn't help but chuckle at the old man. After all the years and dead bodies he had seen, he had to have a sense of humor no matter how macabre, or risk losing his mind.

He knelt down and took a couple of tools out of his case and a pair of gloves. After sliding them on, he reached in and picked up one of the biggest bones in the small pile. This is definitely human. From the looks of the size, I would say very small child, maybe a year or two old. Of course, I'll be able to determine more when I get them back to the office and have a closer look."

"Any idea how long they might have been there?"

"It's hard to tell from just from looking, but if I had to make a guess I'd say about 30 years of so. There are a couple of tests I can do that'll tell me approximately how long it's been there, but it might take a few weeks to get the results back."

"I guess that'll have to do then. I'm just worried that might not be the only one. You know how many kids were

29

supposed to have gone missing over the years from this place."

"I know how many people have spread those rumors over the years. I don't know how much truth there is to any of it."

"After the records I found last year, and some of the things that happened to the kids that were put here, I have no doubt in my mind that the rumors are at least based in some truth."

"I understand it's your job but you, better than anyone, should know some things are better left buried." Dagan looked at the ground to avoid eye contact. He knew Bill was speaking of everything he had found out concerning his family last year. Sometimes he wished he didn't know, and then other times he was glad it had all come to light.

Trying to lighten the situation Dagan teased, "You just don't want all the extra work.

You're ready to retire and go fishing, aren't you?"

"It's getting to be about that time. You'll understand one day." Bill said shaking his head. Dagan helped him bag the bones and some of the surrounding dirt to take back with him for examination. The county was at odds with their budget so there was no extra money for an assistant. Dagan would have to do for now, so he did.

Tony walked over to the pair as they were sealing the evidence bags and writing on them. Dagan made a quick introduction between Bill and Tony.

"I got in touch with some of our recovery specialists. In particular, a man named Dave who is a leading expert on GPR and other techniques. He will be out here in two days. That's the fastest he can get here."

"Thanks. I appreciate it. It'll put my suspicions to rest at least."

The three men spoke a little about what needed to be done to preserve the area and Bill left with the remains.

Dagan and Tony spotted the foreman Adam up near the main building talking to some of the other workers. They headed in that direction, so Dagan could give him the news that for the next several days all demolition and digging in the back area was off limits. He imagined that Adam was not going to be very happy about it. He was right.

"Sheriff I realize this could be a crime scene, but I have deadlines to keep. This job is one of the biggest I have this year and I cannot afford to lose this contract." "I understand and I'm sympathetic to your problem, but these bones belonged to a child. Do you have kids?"

Adam shook his head indicating he did.

"Then how would you feel if this was one of yours? I'll speak to your boss if it helps?"

"It might help, knowing that the order is coming directly from you."

"Give me his number and as soon as I'm back at the office I'll give him a call."

Adam handed Dagan a business card from his wallet and thanked him. He walked off to tell his crew they had they rest of the week off from this project.

Hopefully, the poor guy had another smaller project he could work on in the meantime.

Chapter Six

Thursday morning dawned bright and a tad bit chilly. It would be hot by lunch time though. Although it was early September, the days were already showing signs of being shorter and growing cooler. Most people thought of pure hot sunshine when thinking of Florida's climate, but northern Florida could be quite cold in fall and winter. It even snowed lightly from time to time.

As soon as Dagan returned indoors from taking the dogs out for their morning bathroom break, he put on a pot of coffee. He had been surprised by the cool front that had snuck up on him. He hadn't paid much attention to the weather forecasts lately with everything going on and having a house guest. It was general conversation and then off to bed, instead of the usual hour or so of tv.

For some reason, he did his best thinking right before falling asleep at night, and last night had been no exception. His mind had run scenario after scenario trying to figure out why a baby's remains would have been buried in an unmarked grave behind a children's asylum. It was sad, horrific and unimaginable. Maybe Bill would have some answers when he spoke to him later today. His thoughts were interrupted by Tony walking into the kitchen, showered and dressed to go.

"You're worse than a woman about getting ready in the morning. Here it is time to go to work and you're just lounging around." Tony said knowing how to aggravate his longtime friend.

Dagan shook his head and retorted," Some of us have responsibilities other than ourselves to take care of. Have some coffee while I go finish up. Wouldn't want you to be late to the office."

Tony grinned as he found a to-go cup and filled it to the brim. It seemed as if he and Dagan had never been separated as they had taken different directions in life. He realized now that his friendship had been more like a brotherhood. He had no other siblings, so Dagan was the closest he had come to having one. The antagonizing back and forth they did was refreshing, because the other guys he worked with seemed to have no sense of humor most of the time.

Dagan returned in no time and they headed over to the Oakville asylum to see if the crew had followed orders to cease all operations until they were told otherwise. The place looked deserted. They sat in the cab drinking their coffee for a few minutes and then Tony asked, "What's it like?"

"What's what like?" Dagan asked confused.

"What's it like in there?" he pointed to the entrance of the asylum. They both stared out the front window at a building that could have come from a horror movie set.

"Exactly what it looks like. Creepy."

"You believe in all that ghost nonsense?"

"Not necessarily, but that place right there, it can make you think you're hearing and seeing things that aren't real." Dagan said remembering a couple of incidents that had happened the last few times he had been in there.

"Let's check it out."

"I've already been in there. You go ahead."

"Sounds like you're scared to go back in there."

He looked at Tony with a sideways glance and smirk, "Really? You're going to try the old psychology crap on me. I was in that class with you or don't you remember?"

"I want to go look around. I've never been in one of these old places and I hear they can be very interesting from a historical point of view."

Dagan sighed, turning the ignition off. "Ok. Suit yourself. I'll go along in case you fall through a floor or something and need 911. Or, maybe I'll leave you there, so I can say I told you so."

They walked up the massive front doors of the building, and once again Dagan was shocked that no one had bothered to put any locks on the doors. After the investigation last year when the remains of a young woman were found out here, you would think they would have locked this place up, if for no other reason than to keep the curious out.

The door made a hellacious groan as Dagan pushed it open and stepped inside. It was exactly as it had been the last time he had been here on the night his half-brother Wade kidnapped Dani, when Alice had shot Wade and then herself.

"Would you look at this place?" Tony whistled. He kept turning around and his head pivoted in all directions trying to take it all in.

"Yeah, my first thought too. Then I read some of the records and saw what occurred here over the years. I can't believe they are going to keep this old mausoleum instead of tearing it down. There's a lot of bad that took place inside these walls. I, for one, would not come here for a vacation, no matter how they clean it up and make it look. A coat of pain and new furniture cannot erase the past. Not in my book, anyway."

"A lot of people have never even heard of this place, so they will not think twice about it. You know the history, and that's what has you creeped out."

"I never said I was creeped out. I just have respect for the ones that lived here. And the ones that died here too. It seems wrong to turn this place into a resort when so many people lived anything but happy lives here."

Tony pointed to the grand staircase. "What's up there? I'm guessing it's not Scarlet O'Hara's bedroom?"

"There are patient rooms in a couple of wings, a cafeteria, an old play room. The third floor has more rooms and the old infirmary and morgue is combined. The attic is where all the patient records were kept. I'm not sure if they've been moved out of here yet."

Tony started up the staircase with Dagan following. They came to the nurse station desk and everything was still strewn about carelessly as it had been on Dagan's last visit. The rooms stood open and if your imagination was strong enough you could almost picture the children sitting on the bed, reading or looking out the small filth covered windows, praying that mama and daddy would come take them home soon.

They continued their tour and Tony witnessed firsthand the overwhelming sadness that overcome one that walked these halls. He didn't even know the full story of all that transpired here, but it seemed as if sadness and despair had permeated the air in this place and always would. He was beginning to understand what Dagan meant when he said he didn't understand how anyone could stay here, even after the refurbishment. He peeked into a room that had once been a playroom. An old forgotten teddy bear lay on the floor, missing one eye, and in the corner sat an antique wheelchair. He shook his head in sadness.

Dagan remained silent on this journey to allow Tony to get the full effect of this place. It was not a place of adventure as some had thought. It was a place that should have been revered and respected.

They ascended to the third floor and down the long hallway to the infirmary. Dagan finally spoke up and told Tony that this has been where the remains of the young female had been found last year leading to the ultimate showdown with his step brother in this very same room.

"I haven't been back since that night."

"I'm sorry man. I didn't mean to cause you to relive it all again."

"It's no problem. It's just a bit strange being back here, knowing what happened. I found out I had a brother and lost him right here all in a matter of hours."

Tony could think of nothing to say so he just kept quiet. He looked around for a few seconds and decided to go check out the attic.

As they were walking up the stairs, Dagan said "You know it was the only room locked, except for the solitary confinement room that Wade had kept Dani in."

'I was surprised to find the front doors of this place unlocked."

"It seems they always have been since it was abandoned. Maybe the owners think the

reputation of this place is enough to keep people away."

As they approached the door Tony spoke up," It's not locked today" The door stood open.

They walked in and Dagan experienced déjà vu. The open filing cabinets where he had found Wade's records and birth certificate. The chair over by the windows that he had pulled there to get good lighting to read the records by, and the place he had been sitting when he had read that his father was

Wade's father too. It seemed the air was thick up here and it was hard to breathe. He excused himself and told Tony that he was going back down to get some fresh air. He made an excuse about his sinuses being aggravated by the dust and left. Once outside he felt like he could breathe again. He sat down on the front steps and took in a few breaths of cool crisp air. He was beginning to feel better already.

About a half hour passed and finally Tony joined him on the steps. He sat down beside his old friend with a file in his hand.

"What's that?"

"On a whim, I looked through some of the files. Since the preacher lived here in the area at one time, I wondered if there were any Lockhart's that might have been a patient at here at one time."

He showed the name on the top of the chart to Dagan.

It couldn't be that easy, could it?

"Well, what do you know?" Dagan exclaimed.

"It seems as if the good old reverend was in here for a short period of time. He was put here for ..." Tony searched through the first two papers by flipping the pages, "for lewd behavior regarding young women. Probably the peeping tom thing we saw earlier."

"Is being a peeping tom really lewd? I mean sure it's perverted, but lewd?"

"Back then it most likely was and isn't lewd and perverted the same thing?" He asked grinning.

"Maybe. I don't think commitment into an asylum was necessary though. But from what I've read, children were often put here for much less."

"So now there's a connection between this case and this place. Unbelievable."

Tony took pictures of the records with his phone then placed them back where he had found them. He didn't have a warrant, so he didn't want to take them off the premises. Dagan told him he had taken some last year that had pertained to his case, but Tony was ok with just pictures. He could print them out and use them just the same.

They returned to the office and Tony sat down at the desk that had been set up for him. He was going to print out the pictures he had taken. Dagan walked on to his office to find a small stack of notes left for him. He sat down and started going through them. Nothing urgent stood out. A call again from the man who claimed somebody had rustled his cattle. He just wanted to know if they had found out anything yet. There were a couple of calls from the Chamber of Commerce requesting his presence at the opening of a new grain and feed store later in the month.

So much for that. He placed them back on his desk and looked around for the coffee cup he kept on his desk. Picking it up, he walked down the hall to fill it up. On his way he stopped by dispatch to make sure everything was running smoothly with his deputies and there was no trouble. It seemed it was a quiet day in the county, which was a good thing.

As he was pouring the coffee, he remembered yesterday Dani telling him that the library still had all the old microfiche records of newspapers from the county. Recently they had received a grant allowing them to purchase a program that when certain names and words were input, it would give you the date of a news article that would have information on the names or words you entered. It might be worth a shot, it might be worth nothing.

He walked back out to Tony's desk to tell him that it might be worth checking into. Tony agreed. He asked Dagan to give him a few minutes to return a call to his home office, and look at some reports he requested, and then he would go help him with the search.

Thirty minutes went by and Tony finally emerged from the desk and announced he was ready to go.

The local library was not large by any stretch of the imagination, but it served the needs of its residents. The librarian, Bernice Thomley, took pride in the library where she had worked for the past forty years. She was more than happy to show the two lawmen to the room where the microfiche was kept and instructed them on the use of the new computer program. Once she was confident they understood, she left them to their search telling them she was more than happy to help if they needed her.

The first name they entered was Donald Lockhart. There were no references that came up for his name. Next, they entered his sister's name, Andrea Lockhart.

Again, there was nothing.

On a final whim, they entered the name of his parents, and uncle's name. Still nothing. Dagan gave an exasperated sigh. "Well, I guess that's that."

"It was worth a look."

Dagan reached around the side of the screen to turn it off and noticed that a reference had been generated in the last few seconds.

Gladys Lockhart Dodd, July 18, 1979, Washington County Journal Follow up – August 21, 1979

He pointed it out to Tony "Maybe she's a relative. Let's give it a look-see. Certainly, can't hurt." They flipped through the microfiche until they found the date referenced. When it came around, the headline was astonishing.

DOUBLE DODD MURDER

The headline jumped off the screen in bold black letters. Was it possible there was another murder linked to the Lockhart's name? Tony hit the print button immediately and rolled to another article that was referenced as a follow up to the original piece and printed it too. Both of them had a feeling that they had found the missing link they had been looking for.

Chapter Seven

DOUBLE DODD MURDER
By: Chris Roberts

July 18, 1979

In the early morning hours of July 18, Mr. and Mrs. Oscar Dodd, of 1372 Magnolia Drive in Bonifay, Florida, were found murdered in their home. Their niece, whom they raised, had come home from college on summer break, and was unfortunate enough to find them.

Mr. Dodd was slain as he was watching television, and Mrs. Gladys Dodd seemed to have been preparing breakfast in the kitchen. It appeared as if she struggled to get away from the killer, but sadly did not survive.

The motive remains unclear at the time of this press release. Police have stated nothing of value seems to be missing, this according to the niece, Miss Alice Dodd.

Arrangements for the deceased will be trusted to Bell Funeral Home.

fter reading this one out loud, Dagan then read the second aloud as well.

DODD KILLER STILL AT LARGE
By: Chris Roberts

August 21, 1979

The suspect in the murder of Mr. and Mrs. Oscar Dodd of Bonifay, Florida is still at large. If anyone has any information that can lead to an arrest of the suspect or suspects, their niece Alice Dodd has offered a reward for the capture of her aunt and uncle's killer in the amount of $5,000.

If you believe you have any information that could be helpful, please call the Sheriff's department.

Tony and Dagan sat eating barbecued pork sandwiches at the Blue Caboose, a train themed café beside the train station. The old tracks that ran through town only carried freight trains now. Once upon a time, they carried passengers from this small little farming community out into the big, scary wonderful world, and then back home again.

Tony had read the articles to Dagan as they drove to the café, but they both re-read them as they sat in the booth at the far back corner. They now had a fresh lead to check out. Alice Dodd.

"I swear this is like the most aggravating jigsaw puzzle that I've ever tried to put together. We keep getting one piece at a time, but we have to really dig to find it."

"All the good cases are usually like that."

"Well, I'm about ready to send you back to Tallahassee and get back to my cattle rustlers and speeding tickets."

Tony laughed. "Can't hang with the big boys, huh?"

Now it was Dagan's turn to smile. "It's not that I can't, I've just had enough excitement to last me awhile, and here you show up and I get dragged into another show stopper."

"At least you're not bored. You could be breaking up two old farts fighting over a checker game down at the Cracker Barrel on the county line."

They both chuckled.

They finished up with their late lunch and Dagan dropped Tony off at the office, so he could gather up some things to bring home with him later. He told him he would be back around in about an hour to pick him up then they could head home. Dagan needed to talk to Bill so he made the five-minute drive from the department to the coroner's office. He was curious what, if anything, he had come up with on the remains of the baby found out at the construction site. The receptionist told him to go on back and Dagan tapped lightly with his knuckles on the door. It was already half open, but he didn't want to seem rude. Bill looked up and removed his glasses.

"Come on in, Dagan. Have a seat."

The last time Dagan was here, he was scared. He had brought his sister's dental record to Bill to see if they were a match to the remains of a young woman found at the asylum. Yet one more set of remains connected to that place. It turned out that it wasn't his sister. Her remains had been found in the forest between his house and the asylum, which was directly behind his house if you traveled through the woods to get there. For ten years, she had been so close, and he never knew it. He shuddered slightly, feeling as if a brisk cool breeze had blown across him.

"Amy news on the baby?"

"There's not much I can tell you. Of course, I ran what tests I could, but there was just not a lot left to work with. I would guess the age was two or three-year-old little boy. The poor thing has been in the ground for a very long time. I told you before the tests results come in I thought it had been there for at least thirty years, if not more and it seems that was correct. I can't tell you the manner of death, if it died of natural causes, or was killed. I can tell you the skull was intact with no fractures, so there is that, for whatever good it does. We will probably never know who that baby was or who the parents were."

"I knew there wasn't much hope, so I kept my expectations low."

"It's a good thing you did."

A thought occurred to Dagan as he and his old baseball coach/biology teacher/county coroner sat talking small talk.

"When you were working at the high school, do you remember any students with the last name of Lockhart?"

Bill though for a moment. "Nobody comes to mind. I know none of my ball players for sure. I remember each of you guys as if you were my own kids. There could have been a student in one of my classes with that name. There were students who are memorable, and then there are some who never seem to do anything to stand out or make their presence noticeable."

"It's ok. I was just asking for something I've been working on."

"You know, now that I think about it, there was a janitor at the school that I'm pretty sure was named Lockhart." He tapped his pen on the desk," Lockhart....Lockhart....." he said trying to recall, "David. That's it. David Lockhart. He was there for a while, if I remember correctly. If he had kids or maybe other relatives there by that name though, I just don't recall."

"Thanks Bill. I think that might help." Dagan stood to leave. "I'll check back in with you with you about the baby's remains, or better yet, just give me a call."

"You know I will."

"Thanks, see you later."

Dagan felt a twinge of excitement. He had one more piece to the puzzle. He arrived at the office just in time to check on the shift change and make sure everyone was ok and made aware of what had been going on. After giving instructions to the night shift and discussing some of the people that they had warrants out for, he went and found Tony at his desk. He had already gathered most of his things, including his laptop, and had put it in his bag. They headed home with plenty to discuss along the way.

Dagan told him what he had found from Bill about David Lockhart. They were going to look into that first thing in the morning.

Tony had some reports sent to his laptop that he would open once he got to Dagan's. Hopefully they would contain some useable information.

Once Dagan turned down the red clay road that led to his house, he could feel the tension of the day slowly leaving his body. It always had that effect of him, instant decompression. He knew as he pulled up to his front yard, that the "boys" Kojak and Columbo, would be standing looking out the front living room window. They always knew when he was coming home, no matter the hour. He had learned in a training conference a few years back, that dogs

could smell their master's scent up to eleven miles away. That was one of many things he had learned about their heightened senses, and what made them incredible partners for law enforcement officers.

Tony thought it was funny. "Look at those guys. They know your schedule well."

"They are always right there, no matter where I go, or what time I come home."

"Dogs are amazing creatures."

"Yes, they are. I like and respect them a lot better than most humans."

Dagan pulled onto the pea rock drive with the sound of the gravel crunching underneath the slow-moving tires of the truck. He turned it off and they both got out.

"Can you grab us a couple of beers while I let the dogs out?" he asked Tony. He nodded and headed to the kitchen as Dagan led the dogs out to the backyard to run and do their business. A couple minutes later and Dagan and Tony were sitting in chairs with their feet propped up, sipping on ice cold beer, and watching the dogs play. The rest of the night passed with a few more beers. They temporarily forgot their case at hand and just enjoyed telling stories about the "good old days". Dagan called Dani and she joined them, brining steaks to throw on the grill, and life was good.

The time was coming soon enough, when the puzzle pieces would be many, and they would be eager to put them all together, and maybe figure out the method to one madman's madness.

Chapter Eight

Stepping through the doors of his old high school brought back a flood of memories to Dagan. He could suddenly remember those days as if it had been last week. The lockers being opened and slammed shut were a familiar sound that he had long ago forgotten. Seeing kids hanging around at the locker bays and talking, boys flirting with the girls and trying to talk them into a date for the weekend, teachers standing outside the doors of their classrooms keeping a sharp eye on everyone, those were the good old days. No matter how hard you tried to tell kids that these are the best times of their lives, they refuse to listen. They are probably all just like he was, couldn't wait to get away from the small hometown that had shaped their lives and who they were, who they would eventually become. Nope, just couldn't wait to turn eighteen so nobody could tell them what to do anymore. It took a few years and a certain level of maturity to realize that these were the best days of your life, and you could never go back. He thought he recognized a few faces. In fact, the faces were familiar because they belonged to kids that were the children of the kids he had gone to school with and the family resemblance was showing. There were days that he would give anything to get back. Back to when he was carefree, playing baseball, and his Dad and Rachel were still alive. Those days would never be again.

He spotted the principal up ahead standing in the hallway talking to a couple of students.

Tony just tagged along not being familiar with his surroundings. Dagan could almost chuckle at the curious looks from the students. They were probably wondering if someone they knew was in trouble and he was here to arrest them. The principal had spotted them now and moved towards them.

"Good morning sheriff. What can I do for you today? None of my students are in trouble I hope." Principal Mitchell inquired.

"No sir. Nothing like that. This is Tony Giovanni with the FBI. He and I are partnering on a case and one of the names that came up during our investigation was someone that might have been an employee here years ago. We were wondering if you could help us out with that."

"I can try. How far back are we talking?"

"Late seventies, early eighties."

"Let's go to my office and we'll see what we can dig up, if anything. What was this person's name?"

"David Lockhart. We believe he worked here as a janitor."

"I've only been principal here for eight years, so I definitely don't recall the name. We have had three janitors alone since I started here. It's rare to find someone today who actually wants to work for a living."

"I hear that." Dagan agreed wholeheartedly.

Principal Mitchell searched his key chain for a small key and unlocked a filing cabinet that held employee records. He thumbed through and finally pulled out an old green file folder.

"Here we go. David Lockhart." He took a few minutes to review the file. "It seems as if he was employed here for only two years. September of 1978 through December of 1980. Not much in his record. Seems as if he did his job, no write-ups or anything." Dagan jotted the information down on a notepad.

"Does the school library keep copies of old yearbooks we could look through, maybe get an idea of what he looked like, that is if he had his picture taken?"

"Yes certainly. I can show you two down there."

"No problem. I graduated here, so I know the way." Dagan smiled.

"Ok then, I'll phone the librarian and let her know you're on the way."

Dagan and Tony both shook Principal Mitchell's hand and thanked him for his time, then exited the office. Dagan could've closed his eyes and walked to the library. It is where he spent hours in study hall, not studying anything, except maybe girls. It's where he had met Dani. That alone made the place special.

When they entered the library they found Mrs. Parker, school librarian for the past twenty -five years, in her desk chair at the library counter. She looked up and a huge smile played across her features.

"Well I declare, Dagan Murphy. I never would have thought I'd have you back in my library after all these years." The warmth in her tone relayed her fondness for her former student.

"Mrs. Parker, it's good to see you." Dagan walked around the counter's end and gave her a hug.

"Look at you." She said as she drew back. "Our county sheriff. After shushing you and your friends so many times, I wondered what you might turn out to be, although you were never bad, just talkative." She kidded.

"Mrs. Parker, this is my old college roommate, and Special Agent Tony Giovanni from the FBI. We are working on a case together and we need to look through some of the old yearbooks if that's ok."

Tony shook her hand, "It's nice to meet you Mrs. Parker."

"Likewise." She responded. She turned back to Dagan. "We have every yearbook from the first one published to the current one in the back room. You boys are welcome to look through them." She pointed them in the general direction and then returned to her desk to help a student waiting on her there. Dagan and Tony entered a small room that had several shelves full of yearbooks from years previous. There was a lot of history sitting on those shelves, and Dagan would love to be able to casually look through them all. He had something specific he was looking for though, so he guessed he should get to it.

"Let's see, he said 1978-1980 so I'll grab '78 and you get '79 to start." Dagan handed him the yearbook for 1979. They both sat at a small table and started thumbing through to find the staff sections of each book. Both had a generic picture of the janitor in question. It looked like the same photo, just put in two different yearbooks. Tony stood up and went over to the copier, so he could take the photo with him as a reference. He really didn't see much resemblance between this man and Donald. Family genes must not have been very strong in their family.

Dagan continued to thumb through each section to see if he could find Donald or his sister Andrea. Each grade had the photos alphabetized so it wouldn't be too great a task. He had said nothing about this little search to the principal, lest he ask for a search warrant. Student records were much more protected that just old employees who no longer worked there. Donald Lockhart appeared on the third page of the freshman section. If he had done his math correctly that means his sister would be a senior. He flipped to the senior pictures, but there were nostudents by the name Andrea Lockhart. Maybe she had dropped out, or just didn't attend school here for some odd reason. When Tony returned, he had him look for them in the '79 yearbook. Tony found Donald but not Andrea. Dagan searched the 1980 yearbook, and neither were there.

"At least we know he was here in '78 and '79. We just don't know where his sister was." Tony surmised.

"She could've dropped out or was sent to another school for some reason."

"True. There are too many variables at work here." Dagan replied raking his fingers through his hair.

"I don't see any way around them though, so we just have to keep trudging ahead."

"I know, I'm just frustrated, we get close then the carpet gets pulled a few inches at a time out from under us. We are just going to have to dig deeper. I'm going to run a broad search on surrounding counties to see if I can find any relatives whether direct or distant to the Lockharts. There must be someone else left in the area though wouldn't you think?"

"Yeah, though a lot of old family names are starting to become extinct. Families don't have the number of kids they used to, and if there are no boys to carry the last name, the name fades away as well."

"Still, I think it's our best bet."

"Do what you think will help."

They both said their goodbyes and thanked Mrs. Parker. Once they were back at the sheriff's station, Tony went right to work on those searches he was talking about earlier, telling Dagan he would let him know as soon as he found something, if anything.

Dagan went off to take care of his sheriff duties which today consisted of hearing out several complaints and paperwork.

Tony logged onto a special database that would search for any names being related to the Lockhart name. He checked his notes and remembered he needed to find out whatever he could on Alice Dodd form the article about the double murder. He entered the name Dodd. Nothing to do now but wait.

His phone rang, and he answered. The GPR expert would be here at eight in the morning. He walked over to Dagan's office to let him know.

"At least that'll be one mystery that we can clear up."

Dagan shushed him. "Don't say that very loud. The powers that be will make you eat those words."

Tony grinned. He heard a barely audible beep come from his desk and said," I think I got something." He walked back over to check it out.

The report generated was automatically printed so he took the paper from the printer. The name Mavis (Lockhart) Doyle and along with it, was a file on Alice Dodd that wasn't sealed but wasn't in the public records search either for some reason.

"What the hell?" he said under his breath. Someone had gone to extra lengths to keep it hidden for a reason. He was determined to find out why. He sent that file to print also. As soon as it finished rolling out of the printer he picked it up to give it a look. He couldn't believe what he was reading. He walked quickly back over to Dagan's office but had to wait because he had a deputy in with him. As soon as the deputy walked out he said, "It's a good thing you're sitting down."

"Why?"

"I got a report back on Alice Dodd. It seems someone went to a lot of trouble to keep one of her records out of the public record system for some reason or another. When she was sixteen she had a name change recorded, but it was buried away. Any guesses as to who she was before she became Alice Dodd?'

Dagan sat in confusion and just shook his head no.

"It seems Miss Alice Dodd was a Lockhart before her name change. Andrea Lockhart. I guess we found Donald's sister."

Chapter Nine

"So, we have Donald, who's a serial killer, and we have Andrea, AKA Alice, who found her aunt and uncle murdered under mysterious circumstances. What are the odds?" Dagan was completely surprised by this snippet of information.

"One in a million."

"Do you think she could've killed them and just said she found them? Or, maybe Donald knocked them off?"

"At this point, anything is possible. I'm sure the police questioned her thoroughly, but then again, they would've had no reason to suspect her. She was a college kid coming home for summer vacation. Nothing suspicious about that. Just to be sure though, we can request the records about the case from Holmes County. I would definitely consider him as a suspect given his track record."

"I'll call over there and see about getting a copy of them." Dagan shook his head in wonderment. "I never knew serial killing ran in families."

"Well, we don't know what happened for sure yet, but yeah, I've seen cases where there have been families that killed together for very odd reasons."

Dagan was at a loss for words. He leaned back in his chair and propped his feet up on the box he kept underneath his desk for that sole purpose. "What in the world happened here? Better question is why I haven't ever heard about any of this?"

"You think it might be time to go have dinner with your mom and ask her a few things now that we have more information?"

"It just might. Let me give her a call and let her know we'll be out tomorrow night."

"Sounds good. I was sick of your cooking anyway." Tony jabbed at him.

"I would bet it's better than all that take out you're used to." Dagan defended.

"You would be absolutely right about that, but I bet your mom's cooking will blow yours out of the water."

"You'll get no argument from me on that." Dagan picked up the phone to call her as Tony walked out of the office and back to his desk.

He sat down just staring at the computer screen for a few minutes. This case was turning out to be a real enigma. It had taken him from the Florida Keys all the way to the panhandle of Florida. His perp in the Keys case now has a sister that was somehow related to a family murder. He had to find someone that knew these people and get as much information as possible. He was pretty sure that he had exhausted all the resources he had as far as record searches and not much had turned up from the use of those anyway.

He had spoken to the wife of Donald Lockhart not long after the case in the Keys had been wrapped up and discovered that she didn't know much about his life before they met. He had never introduced her to any family claiming that he had none. The things he had told her about his past turned out to be mostly lies. They had only had one child together, a daughter, which the good reverend sent to her grave along with her boyfriend, because he had found out she was pregnant and decided they were not worthy of this world.

There had to be someone, somewhere that knew him and his family history. He pulled out the newspaper story of the murders and glanced back at it. The last line was the funeral arrangements were being taken care of by Bell Funeral Home. He quickly typed the name into the search engine on his computer and the name, address, and telephone number, as well as a google map with the instructions to find the place were soon displayed. He jotted them down on his notepad and decided that would be his next stop.

Dagan joined him. "I spoke to my mom and she said to be there at seven."

"Great. In the meantime, we need to check out this funeral home." Tony said pointing to the notepad. "It's the one that handled the funerals for the Dodd's. They may have some information that could be of some use."

"Sounds about as good as anything else we have right now. Let me tell my secretary where we're going."

Tony stood up and grabbed a couple of things from the desk and waited for Dagan to join him, then they both walked out of the office. They both stepped out into the bright sunshine that could be blinding at times, causing them both to reach for their sunglasses.

The ride to the Bonifay took about fifteen minutes. Just enough time for Tony to think of a few things he wanted to ask when they arrived.

The historic building stood out amongst buildings that were left empty long ago. This end of the town had once been teeming with people and businesses, but with progress comes change, and the antiquated buildings of the past always fall victim to larger and more modern structures.

They entered the front door to a small chime that broke the eerie silence. They stood and waited as a door to their left opened and a tall older man approached them.

"Good afternoon gentlemen. How may I help you?" He stretched out his hand for handshakes.

"Hi. My name is Dagan Murphy. I'm the sheriff over in Washington County. This is Special Agent Tony Giovanni with the FBI. We are currently working on a case that involves a family member of some people that had services here years ago. We need to find any relatives of the person we're investigating, and this is one of our only leads that could possibly turn up something."

"I'd be more than happy to help any way I can. How far back are we talking?"

"July 1979" Tony answered, after pulling a small notebook from his top pocket and looking at the notes he had written down earlier.

"Well, that's quite a ways back there. I'm sure though we can find the records. My father owned the business before me and he was careful to keep meticulous records. Thankfully he taught me to do the same. It may take me a few hours. Records that old would be up in the attic and I would have to search through them. Of course, they are kept in alphabetical order according to the years, but still that's a lot to go through."

"That's understandable. I can leave you my card and you can give me a call as soon as you find anything." Tony handed him a card with his name and number on it.

"We never did get your name sir." Tony just realized.

"I'm sorry. I'm Jackson Bell." Tony jotted it down for future reference.

"Thank you, sir. We look forward to hearing from you."

The man nodded his head and watched them leave.

"So, what do you make of that? Think he'll be able to tell us anything?" Dagan asked.

"He said they kept meticulous records, so hopefully he'll have something we can use."

"I think I need to start keeping a list of everything we need to do. We have the GPR guy coming in the morning, dinner at my mom's tomorrow night and hoping we hear back from this guy by closing time, which according to the sign hanging by the front door is six o'clock." Dagan took a quick look at his watch. "It is now two-thirty so here's hoping. Not to mention checking on the records here in Holmes County. I sent the sheriff a message earlier so hopefully we'll hear something by the morning."

"I'm determined to put this case to rest, but I just don't know man. If we can't find any other relatives, this thing is going to get shelved. My boss gives me pretty good leeway because he knows how I work, but I'm already stretching this one thin." Tony sounded worried.

"Let's keep our fingers crossed that something will turn up." That was all Dagan could think to say to reassure his old friend.

They rode in silence the rest of the way back into Washington County and to the station. It was frustrating that nothing seemed to be working in their favor, but they both knew that when it comes to cases, that's way it goes sometimes.

The rest of the afternoon Dagan busied himself with departmental duties as Tony waited for the call from the funeral director. Finally, after two hours, his cell phone rang.

"Hello." he answered almost impatiently.

"Mr. Giovanni? This is Jackson Bell from Bell's Funeral Home. You asked me to call you if I found the records you and the sheriff requested. I have them here anytime you'd like to take a look."

"I appreciate it. We'll be back over there in about thirty minutes." Tony signaled Dagan that he had something to tell him.

They said their goodbyes and hung up. Dagan walked over to Tony's desk and they both decided that they needed to get there so they would have time to go over everything before Mr. Bell closed for the evening. Dagan made a quick stop to tell his secretary where he was going but she was not at her desk. He took a sticky note from her desktop and wrote down what he needed her to know and then headed out.

They arrived a few minutes after five, they pulled into the funeral home parking lot. There was only one other car there so Dagan assumed it belonged to Mr. Bell. The walked in and the door to the office on the left was open and they heard Mr. Bell call out and said, "Come on in gentlemen." They both took a seat across the desk from him and he opened a file that had been lying in front of him. "What exactly would you gentlemen like to know?"

Dagan looked at Tony and nodded. He would let him ask the questions, since it was really his case.

"To start with, what was the date of the funerals for Mr. and Mrs. Dodd?"

"Let's see here." Mr. Bell pushed his glasses further up on his nose. "The funeral was held on Saturday July 21, 1979 at ten in the morning. Interment followed at the Still Lake Cemetery out on Still Lake Road. It's an older cemetery that dates back pre-civil war."

Tony was carefully jotting all this information down. "Do you know of any family member, besides their niece Alice Dodd, who may have had a hand in the planning?"

Again, Mr. Bell glanced down and looked through a couple of papers. "I have a name here of Mavis Doyle. I'm not sure if she was a relative. She could have been a close friend of the family. It seems she came in with Alice Dodd and helped her make arrangements, because as it says here "Miss Dodd was very distraught." He glanced up. "I told you my dad was particular with his notes." He looked very proud of that fact.

"We are thankful for your father's attention to detail. We have not had much luck so far. Is there any other information on this Doyle lady such as an address or phone number?"

"There's no number listed but there is an address. It seems she asked that the bills for the services to be sent there. It's 120 Adams Claim Road, right here in Bonifay."

"Well that answered my next question as to who paid for the services. Was there a record of attendance that day?"

"Certainly. We always have a guest book to sign in at the door to give to the family, but we keep a copy for our own records too. I can make you a copy if you'd like."

"That would be great, sir."

"I'll be back in a moment. The copier is in the other office." Mr. Bell walked out of the office.

"So, do you think there's a chance old Mavis might still be around?" Tony asked.

Dagan shrugged his shoulders. "I'd say it's 50/50."

Tony grinned. Mr. Bell returned handing the copies to Tony asking if there was anything else.

Tony asked, "Do you have the plot number of their graves. I am just trying to get all the information I can, cover all my bases so to speak."

"Sure, sure. Let's see, plots one sixty and one sixty-one. If you ever need to find them, you can ask the caretaker and he can direct you to them."

Tony and Dagan both stood. "Thank you so much for your help Mr. Bell. If we have any more questions, we'll be in touch."

"Of course. More than willing to help any way I can." He shook their hands in turn.

Tony and Dagan left feeling optimistic. They were hoping they had just struck the investigative lottery. After they met up with the man coming out tomorrow to use his ground penetrating radar at the asylum grounds, they would pay a visit to Ms. Mavis Doyle. Hopefully, she would be able to shed some light on a few things.

Chapter Ten

Dagan and Tony sat in the patrol truck sipping steaming cups of coffee as they waited for the GPR expert to arrive from Tallahassee.

"You don't think he got lost, do ya?" Dagan wondered out loud.

"It's a possibility, but I'm sure he has a GPS in his car. It's how I found your house. I don't know how any of you get around up here without one. There are so many side roads and dirt roads. It's a wonder you can ever find anyone when you go out on calls. I bet the EMT's and UPS guys just love it out here." He said his voice full of sarcasm.

"I've lived here my entire life, except for my college years. I'm pretty familiar with most of the roads. There have been a few times I needed a GPS to get me where I was going though."

"If I lived here the rest of my life, I don't think I would ever be able to find my way around without one."

Dagan laughed. "That's the way I feel in Tallahassee. The traffic is a nightmare there. I try avoid it as much as possible."

A small red pickup truck came into view down the road that led up to the front of the old asylum where they were parked.

"That's must be him." Tony stated. He opened the door to the truck and climbed down, careful not to spill his coffee. Dagan followed.

The truck pulled up slowly beside them and the driver's window rolled down. Tony walked over and greeted his colleague from Tallahassee. He introduced Dagan to Dave Truman and explained that he had been instrumental in finding and recovering people who had been missing for years, and whose bodies had been buried by the perpetrator hoping that nobody would ever uncover them again. They helped him unload his equipment from the back of the truck, so they could get started hoping it would be a quick task. Dagan was amazed that the GPR looked similar to a push lawnmower. He didn't know what he had been expecting, but he did know it wasn't that.

As they walked around to the back of the building to the grounds where he would begin his search, Dave explained a little of the history of the GPR and how it would work for them. Much to Dagan's surprise, he told them that the use of ground penetrating radar had been around since the Viet Nam war. It had been used to find tunnels that the Viet Cong would dig as ways to hide and plan surprise attacks on the other forces. He added that it was going to be ideal in this situation if they were indeed looking for unmarked graves. It could detect coffins made from wood or metal and could detect vaults that caskets were put in in areas of high-water tables.

"This thing sounds pretty accurate, but how do you know if it's a grave or something else buried?" Dagan asked.

Dave was more than happy to answer his questions. He rarely got to talk about his work and it was refreshing to get to demonstrate it to someone who was curious. He explained to Dagan that graves that were new up to fifty years old showed well defined anomalies on the radar screen. Older graves showed less defined anomalies and could be more difficult for the radar to detect.

"What if it's a body buried without a casket?"

"We can still examine the earth for soil that has been disturbed, or for a trench in the ground which could indicate a burial has taken place in that spot." Dave answered. "There are a lot of times, especially with older burials, that the coffins have disintegrated and collapsed. That can cause a void and its own anomaly. There are quite a few variables"

"This is all really interesting. I'm glad Tony was able to get you to come out here. I really appreciate it."

"No problem. Now if you gentlemen are ready, we'll fire it up and see what we can find." Dave started the GPR and started walking slowly around a small area he had cordoned off with yellow crime scene tape. He had explained earlier that he would makes small grid sections so that if something was found it would be easier to tag to come back to later. He turned the monitor screen on and began to walk slowly in a straight line. He continued back and forth in this grid for about fifteen minutes. He found nothing in the first search grid but was soon working on the next. He was almost at the end of the second one when he got a hit. He stopped and motioned for Dagan and Tony to come look. They walked over and when they saw the screen, with neither being familiar to this type of thing, Dave explained what they were looking at. It just looked like squiggly lines on a graph to Dagan.

"You can tell here that the earth has been disturbed and you can see an outline here of something, most likely a coffin from the shape of it." Dave explained by pointing to certain spots on the screen.

"Guess we are going to have to ruin the construction foreman's day, week, month, however long it takes to clear this up." Dagan said as he removed his hat and wiped his forehead with his forearm, then placing it back on his head.

"I'm going to call and find out what exact measures we need to take in this situation. Dave you keep looking, and I'm going to call headquarters." Tony said pulling his phone out and walking a few steps away. He punched in a few numbers as and then started his conversation with someone on the other end that would give him the information needed to continue this investigation. When he finished and hung up he turned to Dagan and Dave. He told them that Dagan would need to call out the coroner who would need to make a few assessments, which would require digging up what the GPR had hit on. Dagan called Bill requesting he come back out to the old asylum. He explained what they were doing and that the coroner needed to be present. Bill said he could be there in a half hour.

Tony located a couple of shovels that had been left behind by the construction company and he and Dagan began digging. They were careful to take precautions, so they could preserve as much evidence as possible.

Meanwhile, Dave continued to work the GPR looking for other disturbances in the ground. About fifty feet from where they started, he called out to Dagan and Tony. They stopped digging, thankful for the break, and walked over to Dave.

"You see these small indentations in the ground in the shape of a mound that might have sunken in?" he asked as they approached. They both shook their heads yes.

"These are usually a tell-tale sign of graves." He told them.

"Graves? As in more than one?" Dagan asked.

Look around." He motioned with his hand, "Not all older graves sink in, but there are different reasons why some would. I think you may have an old cemetery or burial ground here. The GPR has shown enough anomalies on the screen that I know there are definitely multiple graves here."

"I need you to keep looking Dave, mark each area that you find. Dagan can you call in a few of your people to help out with digging?" Tony instructed and asked.

"This is a lot bigger job than either of us anticipated but it will be a start. What was the remark you made yesterday about me eating my words?" Dagan replied.

"I won't say I told you so, but I told you so. We will wait and see what Bill has to say. I might have to call in the State Archeological Bureau."

"The state what? I've never heard of that." Dagan sounded amazed.

"The state of Florida has an archeological department as well as a state archeologist. We may have to call her in and turn over jurisdiction, if she thinks this situation warrants it."

"Incredible! I never knew. I guess that with all the native American burial grounds around the state and in the Everglades, it would make sense."

"No doubt, it's not something that's well known or gets talked about a lot, but it does exist."

"I guess I should play closer attention to the workings of the state, other than law enforcement." Dagan replied with a grin.

"I think it's just one of those things, unless you have a need for it, you never even think about it."

With that, they returned to watching Dave find spots and places markers on them. Dagan was really starting to have an uneasy feeling. How could this many graves be here, and nobody know about it, or even question what happened to their loved ones? He remembered thinking similar thoughts about the children's asylum. How could someone just drop their child off in a place like that and drive away never to visit or think of them again. It was as if they forgot about their existence. Maybe that was the point, they didn't want to think about an "imperfect" child. The thing that puzzled Dagan the most was not the children and their various illnesses or mental incapability. It was the adults, the ones who were in charge. The ones who were supposed to protect the children and help them heal. He honestly believed, they were the ones who had suffered mental illness. Nobody in their right mind could have allowed children to live or be treated as heartlessly as these poor souls were.

Hopefully, when everything was said and done, the nameless they found out here, would at last be recognized, given back their names and a little respect and dignity that nobody bothered to give them in life.

Chapter Eleven

When the noon sun had risen high in the sky and was now blazing down directly overhead, the small excavation crew needed a break from the mid-day heat. Dagan had called into town and had ordered sandwiches and drinks for everyone and had one of his off-duty deputies pick them up, as well as bring in some tents to set up for everyone to gather under for a respite from the heat.

Bill had determined that some of the remains could be dated back at least 30-35 years, but others could be anywhere from 30 to 70 years or older, judging from scraps of material and things found with the remains. Tony called his boss, who in turn had called the State Archeological Bureau.

Shanice Evans would be out first thing tomorrow morning. She was the current state archeologist and was up to date on newer methods of research and technology. Of course, she could determine that the state had no jurisdiction in this case and turn it back over to the local authorities. It was all a waiting game to see which scenario would play out.

In the meantime, Dagan and Tony would visit his mom tonight and pick her brain about the Lockhart family. Dagan still had to find the time to go interview Ms. Doyle to get whatever information from her that might be of some use.

They spent a few more hours few more hours of digging up graves. Thank God they weren't six-foot deep as graves should be, most of them were only around four foot deep. Whoever had the task of burying these kids didn't even have the decency to bury them at the proper depth.

Dagan set up a law enforcement detail to keep watch all night for the nosy people that might try to get a look. He didn't think it would be an issue just yet, but word gets around fast in small towns. Teenage kids snuck out here constantly to look for ghost or hold seances. He just didn't need that headache right now.

He and Tony headed back to his house where they could take showers, and Dagan could let his dogs out for a bathroom break before they headed to his moms for that promised lasagna dinner. It seemed like ages since he had been here even though it had only been about ten hours. Today has taken a drastic turn that he could have never predicted.

He let Tony shower first, so he could take Columbo and Kojak outside. After spending a few minutes with them playing and running off some energy, he went back in the house to find Tony putting his shoes on. He told him he would be just a few minutes then he went to get cleaned up. He stood under the water stream and closed his eyes enjoying the hot water running down his tired body. He wished he could stay in longer, but he had a dinner date with his mama.

They set out for her house about twenty minutes later and arrived just as she was pulling the garlic toast out of the oven. Dagan walked over and hugged her and then she turned to Tony placing her hands on either side of his face.

"Tony Giovanni, you haven't changed a bit. Well, on second thought, you did get more handsome than the last time I saw you." She put her arms around him and gave him a huge hug

"Thank you, Mrs. Murphy. I was about to say the same. You haven't aged a bit."

Maureen made a waving motion with her hand and said," That's awful nice of you, but I know better."

"Well, you still look the same to me, not old enough to have a son his age." He pointed his thumb towards Dagan. "You look more like his older sister."

"Look out mama, this one is really smooth with the ladies."

"I have Dani thinking I'm hot don't I?" Tony teased with a sly grin.

"She said you were a hottie, not hot."

"It's the same thing!" Tony protested. Dagan gave his buddy the finger behind his moms back causing Tony to laugh and shake his head.

"Boys, sit down and stop your bickering so we can eat this lasagna before it gets cold." Maureen tried to scold but was laughing instead. "Mercy, somethings never change." She said about the times that Tony had come home on short school breaks to spend with the Murphy family instead of going all the way home to North Carolina where his parents lived. She dished out lasagna onto each plate and each of them took a piece of garlic toast. The salads had already been prepared and put by the dinner plates. Dagan and Tony wasted no time digging in.

"You boys act like you haven't eaten in a week." She said amazed at how they were packing it all in.

"We've eaten, just not anything this good." Dagan told her. Tony agreed.

"Tony, what have you been doing all these years since you two graduated?" Maureen asking taking a generous bite of salad.

Grabbing a napkin and wiping the corners of his mouth, he replied "Mostly work. I stay so busy with the bureau that my personal life, or lack there of is nonexistent.

"So, there's no wife, no kids?"

"No ma'am. Not yet. Not even so much as a possibility. I probably would not be an attentive boyfriend. I'm away a lot for work."

"Doesn't look like Dagan here is going to give me grandchildren anytime soon either. I was hoping you had some I could adopt." She smiled at them both.

"Mom, you know if everything works out with Dani and I, grandkids might be in your near future." Dagan interjected.

"Dagan, don't you go making me promises and getting my hopes up if you're not going to keep them." She scolded pointing and shaking her fork at him to get her point across.

"I wouldn't do that to you mama. I am looking forward to having one or two myself. Especially after seeing what I've seen out at the children's asylum. That place was and seems to still be a nightmare."

"I thought the wrecking crew was out there tearing it down and getting ready to build that new resort."

Dagan and Tony looked at each other and Dagan decided to tell her. "They were, but some bodies have been discovered and they are investigating it now to see if they were once patient's or exactly who they were."

"That's awful!" She shook her head in sadness and disbelief. "Those poor children." She touched her hand to her heart at just the thought of what those babies had endured.

"We'd appreciate if you could keep that to yourself for now. We are trying to keep the public away as long as we can." Tony informed her politely.

"Of course. I know how these things work. Don't forget, I had a husband who was a deputy for years and now my son's the sheriff." She said with pride in her voice. "Is that why you came out here? More questions about that place? I told you everything I knew back when..." She trailed off. Dagan and Tony sympathized immediately with her.

"No ma'am. Not at all. It's another case. A family by the name of Lockhart. Have you ever heard of any one by that name in this area? Say around the nineteen-sixties, nineteen-seventies?"

"That name doesn't sound familiar in the slightest." She squinted her eyebrows together as if she were concentrating.

"How about the name Dodd?"

She sat thinking for a moment more and said, "There's something about that name that has a ring to it. I just can't place it."

"There was a double murder over in Bonifay. A woman named Alice Dodd discovered her aunt and uncle's bodies when she came home from college. Only Alice's name had been Andrea Lockhart, but she had it changed after she went to live with them."

"I remember now. I remember that young girl coming home and finding them like she did. It was in all the newspapers at the time. She was around the same age as me if I remember correctly. Do you have a picture of her? Maybe I would recognize her if I could see what she looked like."

"The newspaper article is all we have to go on and there was no picture of her in it. We are going to check out a lead tomorrow of a possible family member and see if she has an old picture that we can get."

"Well if you do, be sure to bring it by and let me see it. I was in quite a few clubs and organizations back then, maybe we knew each other without me realizing it. Her name might have changed if she got married. Of course, the only Alice I remember knowing at any given time was your godmother and ex-boss." She finished out quietly.

"We will certainly get back to you if we get a picture of her. So far, you're our best chance. Nobody around here seems to remember the family, so that means they either kept a low profile, or just weren't the type of people who made a name for themselves in the community."

They discussed a few other possibilities about this unknown family and then went on to more delightful conversation. They had a few good laughs over memories that seemed as if they had taken place a hundred years ago and enjoyed some fresh homemade peach cobbler for dessert. Dagan described himself as full as a tick when they got ready to say their goodbyes and head back home.

On the ride, Dagan thought about how odd it was that they hadn't found any pictures other than the most recent driver's license photo on Donald Lockhart. There had been no drivers license record for Andrea Lockhart, but Alice Dodd had one. The problem was it was just information on an application, no picture. There were no computers or scanners to keep track of all that like the huge databases of today. Not to mention the fact that over the years, things tended to get misplaced.

He got a troublesome feeling in his gut that told him that things were not going to turn out quite the way he wanted them to. There was something his mom had said over dinner that hadn't really struck him at the time but now, suddenly it was all he could think about.

Her words kept repeating themselves over and over.

They were the ones she had spoken about the only Alice she had ever known.

Chapter Twelve

Early the next morning Dagan dropped Tony off to oversee the recovery at the asylum and he went to the office. After a brief check in for the day, he headed over to Bonifay. 120 Adams Claim Road to be exact.

He wasn't sure what he would find, or even what to expect. There was a big possibility that the lady was no longer on this earth and then what?

He found the road via GPS and as was the case with more than most of the roads around here, this one was clay. The orange-red dust would be all over his truck by the time he made it back to the department. He would have to take it out and let some of the trustees that worked around the yard and mechanics shop to wash it.

The scenery never became tiresome in this part of Florida. The long dirt roads, the oaks that hung their arms protectively over those roads, the pines back off in the forest, the massive pecan trees that one could spot every so often growing in the wild. Those were the oldest, taking years to grow as large as some of the ones he had found out in the woods. There were magnolias that grew wild along with mimosa and other flowering trees. The sun filtered through branches giving off a soft glow that made it seem magical.

He knew he could never live anywhere else. This was home and there was a comfort that all this clay and hard wood brought him. He had visited many places in the state on vacations and none of it compared to here.

He soon come to a four-way crossing and saw that 120 was on the right-hand side on the opposite side of the crossing. He pulled through the open gate that had certainly seen better days. He wasn't sure it would even close anymore. It would probably fall off the hinges if anyone tried to move it. The dirt driveway was only about one hundred yards long to the house that sat back off the main road. He could see a couple of chickens running through the front yard as he pulled up to the farmhouse that had probably stood a better part of a hundred years give or take a few. An old yellow tomcat lay sleepily on the porch not giving a thought to the chickens that ran around searching the dirt for a worm to have for breakfast. The tom barely raised his head to look at Dagan as his truck slowly approached the house.

As he got out he could hear the mournful squeaking sound of the windmill out in the pasture as the rusty blades turned slowly in the breeze. He walked down a flagstone path to the front porch and stepped up to knock on the door. He could hear someone walking around in the house and the steps grew louder as they came towards the front door. It made a slight groan as it opened. The little lady, standing about four feet nine inches, stood just inside the opening keeping the screen door closed and spoke through it.

"How may I help you?"

"Good morning Ma'am. My name is Dagan Murphy and I'm the sheriff of Washington County. We are working on a case that may or may not involve a relative of yours and I wanted to know if I could ask you a couple of questions?"

"Pretty near all my people are gone now. I'm about the only one left." She said in a meek voice.

"Actually, a couple of the ones I want to ask you about are already deceased. I just needed some information on them to see if it coincides with some things we've been checking into"

"Who might you be talking about?" She asked raising an eyebrow.

"The Lockharts. Donald to be precise, but we are also looking for his sister, Andrea."

She popped the latch on the screen door. "You might want to come in and sit a spell. I'll get you some iced tea, and I'll tell whatever I can."

He took his hat off his head and stepped inside and watched her as she slowly ambled back to what he assumed was the kitchen for that iced tea. He briefly looked around as he waited for her to return. It looked like any house that belonged to any old lady in the south. The couch and chairs had handmade doilies on the back. There was a picture of Jesus with his hands folded in prayer on one wall, and pictures of a young boy at different stages of life on the mantel of her fireplace. Various knick-knacks, or dust collectors as his mother called them, sat on little shelves here and there and the coffee table has several issues of Guide Post and Better Homes and Gardens. Everything was dust free and very tidy, even if the furniture looked as if it had been bought back in the fifties.

She soon returned and sat down in a rocker directly across from where he took a seat on the couch. He didn't lean back so as not to disturb the carefully placed crocheted doily. He pulled a small spiral bound pad and pen out of shirt pocket, so he could take notes.

He thanked her for the tea then got right down to business. "How exactly are you related to the Lockhart's?" he asked.

"I'm a Lockhart by blood. Gladys, Dale and David were my cousins on my daddy's side. I didn't grow up with any of them. My father and theirs were brothers. My daddy didn't have time for them. He was the oldest of the nine children my grandparents had and was already married and had me on the way before they were barely in grade school."

'So, your families didn't spend much time together?"

"Oh, we spent holidays and such today together. That was enough. It seemed they always had some kid of rift going on between them. Just ain't right for families to act that way, ya know. 'Specially brothers and sister."

"What can you tell me about Dale?"

"Well, he was the quietest of them all. He was one of them men that you think might play ball for the other team, if you know what I mean, but he was married twice and had two young'uns. A daughter with his first wife, and a boy with his second. The first wife wasn't all that bad, she was nice and loved that baby girl Andrea. It was so sad when she died when that baby was only a year old. It surely broke Dale's heart to lose her to the cancer like he did. I don't think he was ever the same after that. He became even more withdrawn if that's possible. He stopped coming around much until he met his second wife Nora. Now, let me tell you son, that woman musta been sent straight to this earth from the bowels of hell itself. He married her about the time that I was getting ready to have my son. Once my baby was born, we found out he had Down's syndrome and she flat out told me that I should take him and drop him off at the godforsaken asylum over there in Washington county. There was no way her or anybody else could've convinced me to put a child of mine there. She was a rude and haughty woman, that one

was. Ain't no wonder Andrea left home and went to live with her aunt and uncle." She leaned forward like she was afraid someone would overhear her even though they were the only two in the room," If you ask me, Nora killed Dale and made it look like suicide."

"When did this suicide supposedly happen?"

"It was after Donald left home. I guess she figured she didn't need him around anymore to help support her or the boy and would be better off without him. Musta had a life insurance policy or something, I don't know. It didn't matter anyhow, she was killed in a car accident about six months later. I said good riddance. Let the devil deal with her."

"Was there a reason why Andrea changed her name when she went to live with her aunt and uncle?"

"I'd reckon she didn't want to be associated with them anymore. They told me it was better for her, so they could get her put on their health insurance and other things. They had a little money and connections with important folk, so it wasn't all that hard for them to do. Not like it would be today."

"When's the last time you spoke with her?"

"The last time I really got to see her and speak to her for awhile was at my boy's funeral. He loved the woods and would walk through them every day. He didn't come back one morning so I went out looking for him. I found him face down in the creek that runs along my property. Nobody could figure out what happened. They said there were no signs of foul play, but I still wonder how he came to be face down in a creek he spent much of his life fishing and swimming in. They found his fishing pole beside him on the ground and it had been snapped in half. It was one more thing they couldn't explain."

She pulled an embroidered handkerchief out of one of her apron pockets and dabbed at her eyes.

"I'm so sorry for your loss Mrs. Doyle."

"It's been quite a few years now since he left, but a mama never gets over the loss of a child, but God gave me thirty years with him and for that I'm thankful."

"Do you have a number or address where I can get in touch with her?"

"I'm sorry son, you're a little late for that. She's gone now. I wasn't even informed of it until a friend of mine had read her obituary in the newspaper and come to tell me about it. I don't get out much anymore."

"Do you have any pictures of her and Donald that we might borrow just so we can have a face to go by in our investigation. We think Donald might have committed some crimes in this area before he moved and would like all the information we can on him and his family, and pictures of the two of them as young people might be of some help."

"I'll have to go through a couple of albums I have with pictures in them, but I can do that and give you a call to come get them in a day or so."

"I'd be much obliged if you did." He handed her a card with his name and phone number on it.

They both stood up and he shook her hand and thanked her for her help and the tea. She walked with him out on to the porch.

"You know, whatever Donald did, it was the direct result of that mama of his. She was cruel to her husband and those kids. She didn't deserve any of them."

Not really knowing how to respond, Dagan put his hat on and said," Thank you ma'am.

Let me know when you get those pictures and I'll be back around to collect them."

He hopped up into his truck and left her standing on the porch. He could tell she hadn't given away all the family secrets, but she didn't have any family left, so for better or worse, she was probably trying to hold on to the last vestiges of family pride she could.

It was time to head over to the asylum to see what they had found. Maybe their search had yielded more results than his had. Something somewhere had to give.

Chapter Thirteen

Tony was seriously rethinking letting Dagan take the interview with Mrs. Doyle and him coming back out here to the asylum. This heat was next to unbearable. He walked over towards one of the evidence tents set up to at least have a bit of shade. The breeze seemed to be picking up now and he thought he could smell the scent of rain. This was not good at all. They would need to set up tents over the sites dug out now to keep evidence from being washed away or destroyed. He heard a vehicle approaching and then a few seconds later a door slam. He turned slightly to get a glimpse of a tall and slender woman headed in his direction. Surely this had to be the archeologist. He watched as she approached with a bag and in one hand and a small briefcase in the other.

"Hello. I'm Shanice Evans from the State Archeological Bureau. I am looking for Special Agent Tony Giovanni."

"You've found him." Tony said extending his hand out in greeting. "Nice to meet you."

"Same. What do we have going on here?" So, she was all business he guessed.

"All these brown cardboard boxes contain the remains we have been finding for several days now. The first remains found were thought to be the only ones and they were of a toddler-sized child. They are currently at the county coroner's office. The thought that there might be more occurred as an afterthought seeing that this used to be a mental asylum for children and young adults, so we came back out with GPR and looked around. Much to our shock, we found all of this and unfortunately, we are finding more."

Shanice peered down into one of the boxes, removing her sunglasses. She then glanced up and around at all the boxes laid before her and asked what steps had been taken when removing the remans.

Tony explained that they had called Bill, the local medical examiner and had taped the area off just as if it was a crime scene, because more than likely, some of them were crime scenes. Each grave had meticulous notes taken on the exact location, and what contents had been found along with the remains. Pictures had been taken to preserve the visual aspect of the position the remains had been found in the grave, then they were gathered and laid out in the boxes as close to the posture that was possible that they had been in the gravesite.

"That's sound perfect. You guys have done the right thing. The only thing for me to do is to determine the age of these remains and see if we need to take over, or if I can turn it back over to you guys and let you figure out what happened here."

"Yes ma'am. Is there anything you need to get started, anything I can help you with?"

"I think I'll be fine. If I need any help, I'll let you know Agent Giovanni."

With that he turned away and walked back over to a site Bill was currently working on. "Do you need a break out of the sun?" he asked as he approached Bill.

"You young'uns today can't handle anything without air-conditioning. I'm fine." His grouchiness indicated that he was not fine. Just the opposite. Tony grinned and offered him a bottle of water out of one of the nearby coolers.

Bill took it and sat down on the edge of the grave he had been working at. He wiped his forehead with a red handkerchief he pulled from his back pocket and then twisted the cap off the bottle taking a big long draw of it.

"Was that the state lady I saw walk up here?" he asked Tony.

"It is. She's over there now assessing what we've found already."

"I hope she likes what she sees and decides to stay. I can get back to my regular job and quit digging around in all this dirt."

"What? I thought you liked all this excitement, playing Indiana Jones and all."

"Boy, I am sixty-nine years old. I've had enough excitement in my life for the both of us. I've been thinking about what Dagan said the other day. I think it's time for me to retire and go fishing somewhere that's far away from here."

Tony couldn't help but laugh out loud at the old man. He wasn't really old, but he played the part well. Bill looked up at Tony, eyeing him with aggravation and retorted, "Let's see you laugh about it when you're my age."

"Come on, you need to sit in the shade for a few, I don't care how old you are. The sun is brutal." He gave Bill a hand up and they walked over to the nearest tent that had a small picnic table under it. They sat on opposite sides and Bill look relieved, but he would never admit it. His generation simply did not admit to a younger one that they weren't tough enough to deal with everyday things like working in the hot sun. Tony let him relax for a few minutes and then pointed towards the tent that Shanice was under. She was currently holding something in her hand, although he was unable to tell what from this distance, but she was examining it carefully.

"What do you think she's going to tell us? "

"She's going to tell us exactly what I don't want to hear. That this is not worth her time or effort and that the jurisdiction is mine. She is going to tell me goodbye and not so much as a "sorry" for screwing up my day. Most of the things I've seen are not older than seventy-five years old. You said unless they were, she would have no reason to stay." Bill sounded exasperated.

"You're right. She will only be interested in things older than that because of the historical value to the state of Florida."

Bill shook his head in disbelief that he was dealing with this. He guessed he had it rather easy as the county medical examiner up until now. It figures that his biggest case was going to hit him when he was ready to retire and just about to the point where he was too old to care anymore. All he could think of to say was, "Well, damn."

~ ~ ~

Dagan called Tony and told him he would be in the office the rest of the day taking care of things he had been neglectful of since this all had started, but he would be around to pick him up as soon as he left for the day, so Tony continued to help at the dig site. They had discovered three more sets of remains and it was nearing the five-o-clock hour. He looked in the direction of the tents where the archeologist was working and saw she was now sitting at a table writing.

He approached the tent and she looked up and motioned for him to sit. He called Bill over, so he could listen to what she had to say. As soon as Bill had joined them, she filled them in on her findings.

"You two certainly have your hands full here." She simply stated as she continued filling out what look like a report form.

"It's that bad?" Tony quipped.

"It's that bad and more. First off, let me start by saying what we have here is not of any archeological significance to the state of Florida, so I won't be taking over this dig."

Bill visibly flinched. Tony held back a laugh. He felt sorry for him.

"Now, with that being said, you guys have a mystery on your hands and I'm not sure how or if it will ever be solved.: She pointed to a row of boxes in the tent behind them. That set of boxes there, are the oldest I've seen, and I would date them at approximately sixty to sixty-five years. The remains of clothing found with them puts them in the style of clothing worn in the late fifties and early sixties. I almost guarantee that testing of the clothing would find the material to be dated to that time frame. Some are even newer than that. I'm sure the hospital had patients that died because of natural causes, but knowing the history of these types of places, I would be more than willing to bet that a lot of these are not natural." She was suddenly interrupted by one of the men who had been digging. He was yelling and motioning for them to come over to see what they had found.

Tony, Bill, and Shanice walked quickly towards the man waving his hand in the air.

"I think this one was buried alive!" he said appalled as they approached. They looked down and, in the ground, below them they saw a nightmare. An astonishing thing not seen many times but seen here and now none the less. There in the space below them was the skeleton of a woman. In between her legs, partially hanging out of her pubic region, was the skeleton of a baby.

Shanice knelt and looked closer. Bill and Tony were simply too astonished at what they were seeing to speak. She stood up after a couple of minutes and said, "She wasn't buried alive. Although it's rare, this is what we call a coffin birth. The woman buried here was indeed pregnant when she died. As decomposition began, the gases filled her abdomen and because she was pregnant at the time of her death, there wasn't enough room for the baby and the gases, so they baby ends up getting pushed out of the body through the birth canal." She said it all very matter of fact and not in the least disturbed by what she saw. "Now when you do your examination, I could be wrong, but that is exactly what coffin birth looks like, so that will more likely than not be your conclusion."

"I've heard about it, but never seen it." Bill said perplexed.

"It's a rare occurrence, but it does happen. Do you gentlemen know of a nice hotel where I can get a room for the night? It's been a long day and I'd love a nice hot shower." She changed the subject as if seeing a dead woman with a baby born after they were both dead was nothing.

Bill looked at her incredulously for a second, then recovered enough to give her directions to a nice Bed and Breakfast on the outskirts of town.

After she walked away, he looked back at the poor souls lying together in that pit. "If that don't beat all."

"It certainly beats anything I've ever seen. I might even have nightmares about this and in my line of work, I've seen some scary things."

"You and me both son, you and me both." Bill responded somberly, then turned and walked away.

Chapter Fourteen

Golden sunlight streamed through the gauzy white curtains of the guest room Tony was staying in. He could see dust motes doing a lazy morning dance in the rays of light that went from the window to the floor. He stretched as far as his arms would let him and yawned, relaxing his arms once again. He tucked his hands in a clasp behind his head and felt like going back to sleep. His muscles were screaming from all the digging and bending he had done over the past couple of days. A hot shower might help, once he decided to climb out of bed.

His mind couldn't think of nothing other than the case he was working. What had begun as a simple investigative exploration into some cold cases, had somehow turned into a whole mess of other things that he was now involved in.

He knew Bill was up to his elbows in remains but had finally been able to go back to his office to begin the examinations.

Dagan had told him last night about the things he was able to glean from his conversation with Mrs. Doyle. It wasn't much, and it was too bad that Andrea Lockhart, AKA, Alice Dodd had passed away. She could have been a great source of information on her brother.

He was amazed that his superior hadn't called him to come back to Tallahassee. He really wouldn't have a good argument to stay. It seemed for every step they took forward, they had to take two back. It must be a slow month for the bureau if they were letting him stay this long without any real results. It floored him that he could find nothing of substance on Donald Lockhart. His life seemed to be virtually non-existent before he moved out of this small town part of Florida. Dagan had told him that the cousin he had interviewed yesterday had suggested that Donald and his sister had led very sad lives, thanks to Donald's abusive mother. She had treated them with contempt and shown them no love, especially Andrea because she wasn't her own. The extent of that cruelty would never be known though, because everyone involved in that tragic mess of a family was gone now.

He decided to get up and head to the kitchen for coffee thinking the caffeine was needed far more than the shower. It was quiet, so he wasn't sure if Dagan was up yet or not. He pulled a t-shirt over his head and opened the bedroom door. He thought he heard voices down the hall. He could hear someone speaking in hushed tones. He continued through the living room into the kitchen. Dagan was sitting at the table, on the phone. He nodded at Tony as he walked toward the coffee maker. Nothing ever smelled as good as coffee in the morning, unless you count bacon frying. After pouring the biggest mug that he could find in the cabinet, he sat down at the table across from Dagan. He reached over and picked up the paper from Panama City to thumb through until Dagan was finished with his conversation. Dagan spoke for a few minutes longer then hung up his phone and put it on the table.

"So, what's on the agenda today" Tony asked him.

Dagan sighed, as he reached for his own cup of coffee and took a big gulp. "Oher than going into the office like I do every day of the week, I don't have a clue. I guess we can stop by Bill's office to see what he has found out if anything. With our luck, that'll be just about nothing."

"I was just thinking this this has turned into one of the most frustrating things I've ever worked on. I should have left well enough alone and forgot the old preacher after I left Key West."

"You and I both know that is not how either of us work. We don't just forget about anything. It hangs around at the edges of our minds and nags us constantly until it takes hold and we can't ignore it any longer."

"True. I just wish something would give, one way or another." He let it go and they both sat quietly as they finished their coffee and read the morning paper before heading into the sheriff's office for the day.

~ ~ ~

The sounds of the phones ringing and the low murmur of voices and laughter was irritating Dagan this morning. He got up and slammed his office door closed, garnering looks of surprise. He needed to be able to concentrate on the budget reports for the fiscal year he was working on and could not summon the focus needed. It was bad enough he had never dealt with these types of things, and now after being thrust into the position, he had nobody to guide him or give him on the job training. He was flying blind and hoped he could get it right. He would have much rather been out on patrol then sitting here in an office doing paperwork. Someone had to do the dirty work and he was the one appointed the job.

A sudden light tap on the window caused him to look up from the stack of papers he had been shuffling trying to make it look like he knew what he was doing. It was Tony. Dagan motioned for him to come in and he waited as he opened the door and stepped inside closing it behind him.

"I am going to head over to Bill's office for a bit. I just wanted to know if you would like to go. It seems you're a bit frustrated with whatever you're working on here." He said pointing to the desk.

Dagan ran his hands through his hair and blew out a breath. "I really should stay here and try to get this done, but to hell with it. If they had wanted a pencil pusher, they should've hired someone other than me."

As they two of them were preparing to leave, Mrs. Della Pipkins, who had worked for the sheriff's department in one capacity or another since before Dagan was born, as a receptionist/human resources/public relations officer/you name it, poked her head through the door. "Dagan it looks like you're off again, but son I have to tell you, the uppity ups have been breathing down our necks, leaving messages wanting to know when those reports there are going to be done."

"Miss Della, I don't have a clue what I'm doing. I am trying but they will just have to wait until I am finished with them. If they don't like it well tell them to go to ... call me." He said changing the ending of the sentence quickly.

She shook her head and asked, "Where are they, on your desk?"

"Yes ma'am."

"I'll look them over while you're gone."

"Are you sure that you can, I mean I'm not saying you can't do the reports because everyone around here knows you basically run this place, but I mean is it ok for you to do that?"

"Son, trust me, I'm no rookie to those reports." She said with a sly grin. Dagan just shook his head and walked away thanking her.

"Don't thank me yet. You still have to look them over and put your John Hancock on them." She called out after him. He turned and gave her a little wave and walked out of the building after Tony.

"Maybe I should tell Dani you're trying to charm the female staff into doing all your work?"

"Yeah why not. Tell her I have a thing for women old enough to be my mother especially the ones who used to babysit Rachel and me when we were little." He replied with a grin.

"There's a lot of that babysitter thing going on these days."

"Dude, you are sick in the head." He said shaking his head back and forth as Tony laughed at him.

It didn't take long to get to Bill's office and they were a little shocked by what they found inside. They were only two exam tables in the room, but they had remains laid out on them as completely as they could be. The others were laid out on sheets on the floor. It looked like a scene from a horror movie and Dagan was just waiting for the army of the dead to rise up and walk out. Bill was bent over a microscope peering at some piece of evidence that had been uncovered after being buried for years.

"How's it coming along Coach?" the term of endearment Dagan used sometimes to remember the good old days when Bill had coached his baseball team.

"It's coming very slowly. I have been extracting samples from the bones and teeth to determine certain pathological conditions and DNA. They will be sent out to the state lab when I'm done and there's no telling how long it will take to get it all back. I'm hoping your FBI friend can get it sped up a bit."

Dagan looked at Tony and smiled.

"His FBI friend will certainly do his best." Tony replied causing Bill to look up from the microscope.

"Oh, you're here too. Nice to see you again. "

"You too, sir."

"We were just stopping in to see what progress you've made, if any. I know it looks like a huge task you have here."

"Huge monumental my ass. More like Mount Everest, monumental, and whatever other words you can come up with. I called for an assistant. They're supposed to be sending one at the end of the week. I believe they found two more graves after we left the other day and so far, no more. Let's all keep our fingers crossed."

"How many in total did they find?"

"Thirty-seven so far."

Dagan let out a low whistle. "Have you made any guesses to it being a cemetery with unmarked graves, or something more nefarious?"

"My own opinion is someone was getting rid of bodies anywhere they could. There was no neat rows or even sections. It was as if they just picked a piece of ground that had not been disturbed before and put the person in it."

Dagan and Tony both shook their head. Logic and decency had very little to do with the things they saw in this line of work.

"Most of these remains belong to children. A few in their early to late teens. Then we have mama over there with her baby. We haven't determined her age quite yet" He indicated with his thumb behind him. "I've only found her and one other adult, but I'm not through examining them all, so who knows what might turn up. The other adult was male and rough guess he was probably in his twenties or thirties. We'll know more when the test comes back. "

"We are going to go back out to the asylum just to look around." Dagan said.

"Well do me a favor, is you find anything else, either hide it or call somebody else." Bill quipped. Dagan laughed and noted Bill's grumpiness was getting worse as he got closer to retirement.

"I had an idea about the records stored there. I called ahead and asked for a warrant just so if anyone shows up representing the owners of the asylum our bases are covered. After finding all these folks, it wasn't a difficult task to get one." Tony offered.

"Sounds good. Let's get on it. It might take a while."

They said goodbye to Bill and headed out to the asylum. It was going to be a long morning going through dusty old records and trying to make sense of what they were looking at or for. The worst part was they had to go back into the building. The very one that Dagan disliked very much.

Maybe today the spirits he swore he didn't believe in would not be restless, or maybe they would be angry because their resting place had been disturbed. Either way, he was about to find out.

Chapter Fifteen

Dagan found it hard to believe he was once again going into the old asylum to look for evidence. It was if this place would never let go of the pain and suffering it had caused when it had been operational. The atrocities committed here were somehow going to live forever it seemed.

He and Tony had already climbed the stairs all the way to the top to find the old records room just as they had previously left it. They were going to search for anything they could find that might have mention of the deaths that occurred here. They would be very lucky if they could find anything. The way those remains were recovered, it wasn't like the people who ran this place cared what happened to the patients in life, much less in death. Dagan still had the box he had found in his mother's attic that had belonged to his aunt who had once been a nurse here. He had used it to help solve the case that involved his missing sister and found out through the letters and notebooks in that box that he had a half-brother that had once been a patient here. That half-brother had tried to kill him and Dani but ended up being killed by his birth mother Alice, who just happened to be the sheriff and Dagan's Godmother. He had looked through its contents last night but could find no mention of any one specific death, just an overall disgust his aunt had for the way the children had been treated. She ended up quitting her job over it.

Tony handed him a box and then grabbed one for himself. They went and sat closer to the windows for the light in some old office chairs that had been stored up here at one time. Time seemed to drag slowly as they scanned through file after file. It was stuffy, so Dagan managed to get the old window open after quite an effort and propped it open with an old wooden ruler that he had found on the floor. At least there was a nice breeze flowing through and he felt like he could breathe easier. The morning hours had given way to early afternoon when Tony finally spoke breaking the silence.

"Ok, we might have a hit here." He was still looking over the paper he held in his hand when curiosity got the better of Dagan.

"Are you going to tell me or make me guess?"

"This letter seems to be from a woman, Ginger Barnes, whose daughter had been placed here by her father for reasons, and I quote, *better left unspoken*. She was worried because she claims her daughter wrote her regularly, yet she hadn't heard from her in several weeks. She was writing this letter to ask if she had taken ill or, if not, was there some other problem as to why she had not received any letters from her."

"Is there anything to indicate someone responded to her?"

"No, but if she wrote this letter, maybe she wrote more. I found it in this box, so I'll keep digging. It says her daughter's name was Lyric Barnes."

"I'll go look through the patient records in the filing cabinets and see if I can find her name and files."

Tony nodded his head at Dagan, then started digging through the box once again.

Dagan made his way to the filing cabinets that had revealed old family secrets to him not so long ago. He was almost hesitant to look through them again. What other secrets that other families harbored might turn up? He opened the cabinet that was marked with the letter B and thumbed through files after file carefully so as not to miss anything. He really hated having to backtrack and repeat something. He found the file he was searching for and pulled it out of the drawer. He let Tony know what he had and went over to the window to look through it. There were several pages explaining that she was a sixteen-year-old female and that various tests had been run prior to her admission. There was a list of said tests and various medical mumbo jumbo. He scanned the papers for the reason for admission. Some of the reasons he had discovered for these children thus far had been utterly ridiculous.

Near the bottom of the page he found written in faded red ink: *Erotomania and female troubles* as the cause of her admission. He wasn't a woman but knew that female troubles could mean a myriad of things, none of which he thought would warrant being institutionalized in an asylum. He had never heard of the term erotomania, so he pulled out his cell phone and googled the definition. He found a dictionary site that described the word as meaning a condition in which a woman believes a person is in love with her if that person shows the least bit of attention. He thumbed through the papers following that one and read that she had psychological issues causing her to present herself as a wanton young lady. Dagan couldn't help but shake his head. Her admission and the treatment following it that she received was most likely ridiculous. This young woman had probably been more flirtatious than her parents or others thought proper and they had put her here to rectify the situation. What a time that was to be alive. If those folks could see the way young people acted today, they wouldn't be able to build enough of the places to house them all in.

"Tony, this record indicates that she was put here for erotomania and female troubles."

"Eroto what?"

Dagan explained the meaning of the word and then continued," Now, according to what else I read they said she was wanton, in other words she was a little flirtatious and maybe a bit of a tease, who knows, but it makes me wonder. If this report is the same girl that matches with the mother's letters about her daughter not contacting her for several weeks and we can find more letters supporting that, then we might have the ID of one of our victims."

"Victims? Is that what we're calling them now?"

"Don't you think it's more than likely that's what they are?"

"There's nothing yet to indicate they were murdered, but I can understand why you're leaning in that direction."

"Being in this place for dumb ass reasons like those I've found in these records tells me that there wasn't one child placed here that wasn't a victim of something."

"I agree, but that doesn't mean they were murdered. We have to look at it from an objective view point, you know that."

"Yeah, I know, it's just hard given what we know so far."

Tony called out several other names of children that had various maladies that might have caused death, therefore could have possibly been buried in the back yard of the asylum. Dagan pulled those files and placed them in a box to go through later.

"I found this record that is really sad. It indicates there was a child here that had severe pneumonia and the treatments did not seem to be working. There is a note from the doctor stating they had contacted the child's father and he had responded to do whatever was necessary, but he would not be able to make it out to see the child. He had important business to attend to in the capital. The father also requested this information be kept from his wife as she was very easily upset by the notion of the child having to be placed in the asylum."

"Wow, another candidate for father of the year This happened too often. They would place them here away from the world so that society would not judge them for having a less than perfect child, and then just forget about them. If the worst occurred and they had to give them a proper funeral, it would have made them face what they had done, so they just let the asylum handle it." He sounded so disgusted.

"See if you can pull his file. His name was Aaron Lyons. He was only 4 at the time he was admitted. If we can find any living relatives to swab for DNA, we might be able to identify these kids and give them a proper burial. It would be the least that we could do for them. He sounds like a good match for that first sets of remains that were found."

Dagan went back to the files and searched for the cabinet that had the letter L. Upon opening the drawer, a strange feeling hit the pit of his stomach. He couldn't identify the feeling, but it was probably hunger mixed with being hot up here in this stuffy attic. He should tell Tony that they needed to break for lunch soon. These records had been here all this time, they certainly weren't going anywhere.

He was scanning each name looking foe the last name of Lyons, when he came across a name that was familiar.

Lockhart.

Tony had found his file days ago but had placed it back in here before they had left that day. He pulled it out anyways, so they could go through it. They had a warrant, now they could take them off premises.

"I found the Lyons kid and also found Lockhart's file that you had the other day."

Tony gave him a puzzled look. "I didn't take his file from that cabinet and I didn't put it back in there. I found his file on a stack over there by the wall. I never looked in the filing cabinets. I thought it was strange that we were working on his case and there was a file here on him just laying out in the open like that. I thought is was just a coincidence." Tony walked over to the stack he was referring to and found the file he had looked at several days ago. He held it up for Dagan to see. "This is the one I found."

"Why would he have two separate files?" Dagan asked flipping the pages.

"Well this one is pretty thick. Maybe they needed to start a new one. I say we take them both and go through them later. We know he is not one of the unfortunate few from out back, so we don't have to worry about using the information to try and identify him."

"Sounds good. Are you about ready to take a break? I'm starving and could use some air conditioning about right now. It's getting really hot up here."

"Is that what I smell? I thought it was the old mustiness of the attic and it was you all along."

"I'm so hot I can't even think of a retaliatory comment right now."

Tony laughed at his old friend and they carried a couple of boxes down and out of the asylum. In total they had found seventeen files so far that were good candidates for the remains they had recovered.

"I think we should give Bill a call and tell him what we found. He might have a few ideas of what we need to do to try and match these records to the deceased." Tony advised.

"I'll give him a call when we go in to the office later."

For now, the two of them would grab a bite to eat and cool off. Fate would smile upon them today and give them a small break. Two of the records they had found were for former patients that were tied together in life and in death.

Chapter Sixteen

Bill sat down at his desk and leaned back in his chair as far it would allow him to. He was nearing the brink of exhaustion. The sheer size of the task he had undertaken over the last few days would've been intimidating for him as a younger man, one much less nearing his retirement date. He had called for help and the state had sent two assistants to help with whatever he required. He had only been expecting one so there was that little bit of good. At least for now, he could take a short break and let them handle the rest. He was in desperate need of coffee but didn't smell it brewing the way he could most mornings. That most likely meant that the receptionist Shelly was not in yet.

He let out a small sigh, then heaved himself up out of the chair to make his way towards the employee lounge. The *lounge* was just an empty records room that Shelly had set up a coffee pot, small refrigerator, and microwave in. There was also a small table with four chairs for anyone working there that might need a break, and a place to eat their lunch.

He emptied the grounds from the top of the maker into a nearby garbage can and refilled it. He was not sure how many scoops would make a decent pot, so he just guessed. There were gallon jugs of water sitting in the corner, so he got one and poured the water into the tank to the fill line. The pot itself looked clean but he walked across the hall and rinsed it out in the bathroom sink just to make sure. Placing it back on the burner he had just pushed the on button when he heard someone walk up behind him. Turning his head slightly he noticed Shelly putting her things on her desk and rushing into the room.

"I'm sorry I'm running a little behind. My ex never showed up to take the kids to school, so I had to run around to three different schools to drop them off. Guess that's what I get for having them so far apart. One in elementary, one in middle, and one in high school. I'm already tired and the day hasn't even started yet."

"It's fine. I just hope I haven't screwed up the coffee too bad."

"I'm sure it's ok.' She said with a half-worried look. The last time he made coffee they could have used it to revive the dead stored in the back.

"If it's not, just dump it out and start over." He said with a smile. She grinned and walked out to her desk, so she could get her things organized and start entering all the information he had given her so far on the remains that were being sent off to the state.

He thought chemical isotope testing would give them a clearer picture of where some of the children had lived or at least came from. He did not have the proper facilities to do the testing here, so he had to send them to the state lab to have it done.

He walked back to his office and sat down in his chair. The coffee would be ready soon enough, so he picked up the phone and called his wife. He hadn't seen much of her in the last few days. It rang several times but there was no answer. She was probably at one of her club meetings or something.

She belonged to the garden club, the quilting club, and several others he couldn't remember the names of right off the top of his head. She had retired from teaching several years ago and he was very eager to join her. She had become a member of all those clubs to busy herself while he still worked. Once he retired, she told him she wanted to travel and see the country. It sounded better and better every day.

He picked up the phone and placed another call to the sheriff's department. He left a message for Dagan that he needed to see him whenever he got a chance. He would explain to him what he was doing. There was not a lot he could conclude from all those remains, but he was certainly doing whatever he could to get the best and most reliable information possible.

He had put in a call to the local newspaper asking for anyone that might know or be a relative of someone that had been a patient at the hospital to contact him. He would ask them if they were willing to give DNA samples to see if they could try and identify any of the remains that way. It was a long shot, but he figured he would use every avenue to try and get the case resolved.

Thirty years ago, he would have been doing somersaults to get a case like this. It had the potential to be the biggest case of his career.

Now, he just didn't care.

His dad had told him years ago, when you come to a point in your life that your job has no meaning anymore, it's time to move on. He had missed out on so much with his wife. She had stuck by him although she spent many nights alone as he worked, never complaining and always with a smile on her face to greet him after a long day or night of work. He certainly didn't deserve her. They never had children and that had been painful for them both. He supposed it would have helped ease her loneliness, but he knew it might have made things harder. It was time he gave his wife everything she had sacrificed so he could do this job over the years. It was time for her to have his undivided attention.

Right then and there he made a decision. This was it, he would be out of here as soon as this case was finished.

~ ~ ~

Dagan had received the message from Bill to come see him, so once he checked in with his deputies that were on duty and others in the office he headed over. He was met by Shelly coming out the lounge with a steaming cup of coffee in her hand. She asked if he was there to see Bill and he nodded. She then asked him if he would mind giving the coffee to Bill. He walked in to Bill's office stating, "Shelly asked me to give this to you, and Good Morning by the way."

"God bless her, and good morning to you too." Bill said as he took a long draw off the coffee. He didn't even care that it was hot and burned his tongue and throat going down. He immediately took another sip, before placing the cup on his desk, knowing he had just made the most awful coffee in the entire world.

"You said you needed to see me, here I am." Dagan took a seat directly across from him.

"Just wanted to fill you in on what I'm doing and have done so you know where we stand in this investigation. I took out an ad in the newspaper asking anyone that had a relative in the asylum to come in and give a sample of their DNA. It's a bit of a stretch but it might work, you never know. I also have prepared some of the remains to be shipped to the state lab this afternoon for chemical isotope testing."

Dagan raised an eyebrow. "You act like I know what that is."

"Well, because bones and teeth are the hard parts of the body they are typically all that's left after a long while. Bones can tell us things about the last twenty to twenty-five years of a person's life such as where they lived and if they lived in different geographical locations or stayed in one place their entire life. The isotopes can be used to determine what their diets consisted of and what water sources they drank from. For example, well water versus city water. I could go on but a lot of it is medical mumbo jumbo that you probably aren't interested in."

"I don't care what methods you use. I just hope something works. If for no other reason than to give these kids a proper burial and resting place. We found the records for a sixteen-year-old girl the other day that might be a fit for the remains of the young mother and baby. As soon as we have something we can compare it to, I'll bring those over."

Bill nodded his head, then changed the subject, just plain tired of talking about it. "I might as well tell you first, I have decided this is my last case. After this is cleared up, I'm retiring."

Dagan sat speechless for a moment. "I can't say I blame you, but I'm going to miss you. I have never worked with anyone else. It might be a hard road for a while."

"You'll get used to someone else and you'll both do fine."

"You and I go way back, back before any of this." He said sweeping his hand around. "You were my biology teacher and my baseball coach long before I became a deputy."

"I remember", he smiled fondly. "I worked the school in the daytime and here at night and on weekends. I'm tired and just want to spend the rest of my days fishing and seeing the country with my wife. I feel like I haven't seen her in years, yet we see each other every night."

"If anyone deserves it coach, you do. As sad as I'll be to see you leave, I'm happy for you." Dagan said and really meant it. He hugged the old man that had earned his respect many years ago. He had been Dagan's teacher, coach, colleague, and a second dad.

Bill seemed to have tears in his eyes and quickly looked away from Dagan. "Umm, as soon as I hear anything from the state, I'll let you know."

"Yeah. That'll be good." Dagan managed after a lump suddenly developed in his throat.

"I guess I'll get back to the office and do some sheriff type stuff." He said to lighten the mood.

"Boy, let me tell you something. You're a deputy and a damn good one. You weren't meant to be sitting in an office no matter what the title or pay is. Do what makes you happy. Life is too short."

"Yes sir." With that, Dagan walked out of the office. If Bill had ever had a son, he would've wanted him to be just like Dagan.

Bill picked up the phone and called Shelly at the front desk. He asked her to call the florist and order him a dozen pink roses and have them sent to his wife. He was going to give her the news tonight of his retirement. The thought gave him renewed energy, unlike that awful cup of coffee he had made this morning. He had let it grow cold sitting on his desk hoping that Shelly would make another pot.

He whistled as he left his office to go back down the hallway to resume his examinations of the asylum remains, leaving Shelly and the rest of the staff staring at him in shock.

He couldn't help but laugh.

Chapter Seventeen

Through diligent work and some dubious computer skills attained from a co-worker, who Tony was certain had more than enough knowledge to bring down the internet, he managed to find out that the mother of Lyric Barnes, the sixteen-year-old whose records they had found in the asylum attic, was still alive and currently residing at the Sunny Days Nursing Home in Marianna. Since that was only a thirty-minute drive down I-10, he was putting that at the top of his list today.

Dagan hadn't returned from Bill's office yet, so he would wait a while longer to see if he wanted to join him or had other things on his agenda for the day.

He had put in several requests to his home office for information regarding the Oakville Children's Asylum. It had been run by the state of Florida so there were bound to be records that might give them some insight into the daily operations of the place. If the records had been kept and handled properly by the state, that is. He figured it was a fifty-fifty shot.

He began to regret what he had asked for when he heard his computer start making that pinging sound it made every time a new email come through. It seemed as though it pinged every five seconds and continued for the better part of a half hour or more. He finally had to mute the notification sound before *he* needed to be placed in an asylum. Not to mention the looks he was receiving from others in the office. None of them were quite sure what to make of the FBI man, but they knew he was good friends with the Sheriff, so they were friendly enough towards him.

"Sorry guys." was all he managed to say looking sheepishly. He figured he would wait until all the files had come in before he started going through them, so he took the opportunity to get a soda from the machine in the break room. It felt good to stand up and stretch a bit before returning to what he was sure was going to be more than a few hours of reading and searching through records.

He sat back down and made the plunge. He opened the first of many emails that had all the information that he had requested and began downloading the various files to his desktop. He would then save them on a flash drive that he could take back to Dagan's later and let him go through them as well. As a matter of fact, he would make two copies so that Dagan could keep one and they could search simultaneously, with two pairs of eyes being better than one.

Just a casual glance as each one downloaded and he opened it up to save it brought about an information dump of inspection records, the company's private accounting ledgers, a doctor's attendance book containing notes from meetings, photographs and ledgers containing patient's information such as their admission and release dates as well as their patient numbers, who had them admitted, etcetera. Someone back in the home office was laughing furiously at him knowing he had asked for it, but not knowing what he was going to get in return.

He blew out a big breath and decided there was nothing to do but dive in. He had just begun to look through the dates of the meetings that took place for all doctors and nurses when Dagan came back. He silently thanked God that this task would be dealt with tonight and he would have help to do it.

"You have a serious look there buddy. Lighten up." Dagan teased.

"You might rethink that when I tell you what all I have here, and that you're going to help me sort through it all."

"What? When did you become the boss around here?"

"I could pull rank, but I'll reserve that for later. Right now, I am going to Marianna to see Lyric Barnes' mother. Apparently, she lives in the nursing home in Marianna. I was waiting around to see if you wanted to go."

"Yeah, why not? I hate sitting around in this office. I can't wait for elections to roll around. Maybe I can get my old job back."

"You mean you're not going to keep your position as sheriff? You're not going to enter the wonderful world of politics?" Tony said with a smirk.

"I'd rather run through hell in kerosene-soaked underwear."

"Don't hold back, tell me how you really feel."

"Let's go." Dagan replied with a smile.

~ ~ ~

I-10 was always busy, it seemed, not matter what time of day it was. They only had a thirty mile stretch to drive until they came to the exit for Marianna. Dagan followed the flow of traffic as several cars in front of him was taking the same exit he was. He wasn't quite sure where the nursing home was located, so he had programmed the address into the GPS and was following the instructions. According to the map, it wasn't too far from the exit they had just taken, only about two miles.

The entrance to the nursing home looked just like the entrance you would see to any other healthcare facility or doctor's office anywhere. The receptionist at the front desk greeted them with a friendly smile and asked if she could help them. Dagan showed her his badge, as did Tony, and they asked if they could visit with Ms. Ginger Barnes. She had a concerned look on her face and thought she might need to call the administrator. She buzzed his office and he came quickly down the hallway to assess the situation. He was a short, stout, balding man who had a perpetual look of someone who thinks that everyone is out to get him. He seemed rather nervous that two law enforcement officers would be here to see one of his residents.

"Can I help you two gentlemen?"

"We're here to visit with Ms. Ginger Barnes." Dagan answered.

"Is there a problem? Are one of you related to her?" he said out of concern having seen their badges.

"None that we know of, and no we are not related to her. I can see we need to put your mind at ease Mr ...." Dagan paused waiting on a name to go with that mister.

"Mr. Walker. I am the Administrator of this facility."

"Mr. Walker, we are here to talk to Ms. Barnes concerning something that happened a very long time ago. It's in reference to her daughter."

"I happen to know she has no children. Are you sure you have the right person?"

Dagan looked at Tony for a brief second and Tony's expression was one of agitation. He was glad he was the one doing all the talking.

"We're sure. Her daughter died at a very young age, but recently we have had things come up that could be related to the circumstances surrounding her death and we need to ask her a few questions."

"Well, I guess it'll be alright. She has no family to object, but if she seems to become agitated I must insist that you gentlemen respect her and leave her be."

"Certainly. We don't want to upset her, we think she may have some information that could clear a few things up."

"Come with me, I'll take you back to her room."

They followed him down a main hallway that split left and right at the end of the main corridor. They turned left and walked all the way down to the end of that hallway that ended with a large exit door.

"We have her here close to the exit. We put all of our patients most likely to need an ambulance here so the EMT's can get in and out a lot faster with their equipment."

"Is she that fragile?" Dagan asked now worried that the questions might indeed send her into a medical emergency.

"She has lung issues. She's on oxygen but there have been several times that hasn't been enough, and she needed to be rushed over to the hospital."

Dagan nodded that he understood, and they pair followed Mr. Wilson to her room. The door stood wide open, but he tapped very lightly to gain her attention.

The old lady sat with her back to them staring at the window that overlooked a small meditation or prayer garden. She seemed to be watching a young family out there with an older male resident sitting in a wheelchair. They must have come to visit and were spending time with him outside in the sunshine and fresh air.

"Excuse me, Ms. Barnes. You have two visitors that would like to speak to you."

She turned her head slightly and stared at the three men for a moment, then turned back towards the window without saying a word.

Mr. Wilson just gave them a *good luck* look and left them alone.

Tony and Dagan looked at each other and Tony shrugged his shoulders. He motioned towards Ms. Barnes as if to say are you going to talk to her, or should I? Tony mouthed "you're the sheriff", so Dagan took the initiative and walked over closer to where she sat.

"Umm, hi Ms. Barnes. My name is Dagan Murphy. I'm the sheriff of Washington County. This here is my colleague Tony Giovanni." He pointed to Tony as he stepped into her line of sight. She glanced at the two of them but didn't say anything.

"There's no easy way to tell you why we're here so I'll just be straight forward. Recently some remains were uncovered at the Oakville Children's Asylum. We have some reasons to believe your daughter may have been...." He paused briefly, "one of the recovered."

She looked up at him. "Why?"

"Why what ma'am?"

"Why do you think it could be my daughter?"

"Well, we aren't sure of anything at this point, but her records stated that she had passed away in the asylum one year after being admitted there. We researched her name in the database of graves around the area, we noticed she was not interred in any graveyards or public cemeteries. Was she buried on your private property perhaps?"

"NO." she said forcefully. It startled both men and they shared a confused look.

"Can you tell us where she was buried then ma'am."

"My Lyric was a beautiful girl. From the time she was born we knew she would be a great beauty as she grew older. There was never a shortage of young men coming around to call on her. She was a bit flirtatious but no more so than any other girl her age. Her father caught her sneaking out one night to meet a young man on the front porch. She swore they weren't going anywhere, just to sit on the porch but that was enough for him. He didn't care one bit about her reputation, he was worried about his own. He put her in that vile place." Her tears started rolling down her cheeks. "She didn't deserve to be locked away like some crazy person. She wasn't crazy, just too beautiful for her own good, but back then women and girls could be admitted by their father or husband for the most ridiculous of reasons. I was threatened plenty after he put our girl there. He often asked if I would care to join her."

Dagan knew if the man had stood before him right now he would have probably punched him. "I'm so sorry for your loss Ms. Barnes. Do you know if she was buried there?"

"My husband told me that she had been buried in the small cemetery there. He didn't want her in our family plot. I never forgave him and the day he died, I let him know it."

"This is a hard question to ask you Ms. Barnes. The set of remains we found was of a young woman the same age your daughter would have been at the time. The only thing is, she had been pregnant. We found the unborn child with her. Is it possible this was your daughter?"

She remained silent for several moments, staring down at her hands that lay folded in her lap. "I guess anything is possible. I know she had met a young man at the asylum that she had really taken a liking to. He was there for reasons as stupid as the one they come up with to put her there. She wrote me several letters telling me about him, and about the plans they had made for when they got out. I knew it would never happen. Her father wouldn't let it, but she had to have something to dream about and keep her going inside that place."

"You wouldn't happen to remember his name, would you? We would like to collect DNA from as many living relatives as possible of anyone that had a relative there, so we can try to identify the remains of the others we found."

"There are more?"

"Yes, ma'am, quite a few."

She sighed a heavy sigh. "I don't recall his name. That was so long ago. My memory isn't what it used to be."

"Do you still have any of the letters she wrote you?"

"No. Again, my husband....." she left off.

"Do you mind if we get a sample of your DNA? It's painless. Just a swab of the inside of your cheek with a cotton swab."

"Fine, if you think it will help."

Tony busied himself opening the swab kit and preparing it, then walked over and took the sample they hoped would shed some light.

"Thank you for your time Ms. Barnes. If you think of anything that might help, please call us." He reached over and took her hand in his, patting hers on the top. He handed her his card. She stared at it for a moment then put it on her bedside stand.

She turned away from them and stared out the window once again.

Chapter Eighteen

After three hours of digging through the reports and patient records that Tony had received yesterday from the state, he decided to take a break. There really wasn't much information there that could be used to help determine the identities of the dead, other than the records that showed the patient's name and who had them committed. They could use these to try and find living relatives.

Tony was beginning to understand why Dagan had no desire to go back into that building. Some of the excuses he had read for these kids being admitted were restlessness, fright by a dog, mental exhaustion and melancholia. The one that infuriated him the most though was *stupid*. Someone had labeled children *stupid* and had them admitted for it. How was that even a diagnosis?

People were so ignorant and barbaric back in those days. He had to walk away from all of this for a little while. He told Dagan he was going to get a sandwich and walked out to the kitchen to decompress.

He took the deli meats, cheese, lettuce and tomato, and condiments out of the fridge and sat them all on the counter.

He could hear Dagan's phone ringing in the other room, then heard him talking. He went ahead and made two sandwiches and walked back into the living room with them and two beers. Dagan was hanging up as he walked in the room.

"That was Mrs. Doyle. She found those old pictures she said she had and told me I could come get them at my convenience. I'm thinking about running over there in the morning."

Tony handed Dagan a sandwiches and beer and sat down on the couch.

Dagan thanked him and took a big bite out of it not realizing until that moment how hungry he was. He held it up and said thanks. The two of them sat in silence as they ate. They never spoke a word as they finished their beers either. That was the great thing about men. They could be in the same room for hours and never feel the need to talk. If Dani had been here, she would have had something to say after every bit and every sip. He loved her but appreciated his buddy's silence. He was going to miss his old friend once he was gone back to Tallahassee and made a vow to keep in touch and get together with him more often. He was the brother he wished he had growing up.

"Kojak, Columbo, let's go outside." He said finally breaking the silence.

Tony told him he was going to dive back into the records and Dagan nodded. It was going to be a long afternoon.

~ ~ ~

When Dagan arrived at Mrs. Doyle's house the following morning, she was sitting on her front porch. He guessed she didn't get much company, so she was waiting on him. She had a small shoe box beside her on the swing. She took it in her hands as he walked up to the porch.

"Good morning." He called out.

"Good morning sheriff. I have the pictures put in a box for you. I would like them back when you're done with them."

"Of course. We just need to look through them. If there are any we think are significant, we'll make a copy. I will get these back to you as soon as possible."

"Oh, no hurry. They've been put away for years now, but it is all I have left of some of my kin."

"I understand. Pictures can be very precious after our loved ones are gone." He thought of the pictures of his sister and dad in his living room.

"I labeled them best I could. I put the names, dates and such as best I could recall on the back of the pictures to help you out."

"I appreciate it ma'am. I'm hoping to have all this wrapped up very soon and then I'll get these straight back to you."

"Like I said, no hurry. I ain't going nowhere unless the Lord calls me home."

Dagan suppressed the urge to grin at her statement indicating she had a boring life. "Yes ma'am. Guess I'll be on my way then. Again, thank you for your help."

She nodded her head and he walked back to his truck. Hopefully there was a clue somewhere in those family photographs. Who knew? It was a long shot, but one worth looking at, especially when you had nothing else. The thing that bothered him most was there were a lot of long shots taken lately. They ended up leading them to the next one instead of helping them find closure.

~ ~ ~

Maureen Murphy could hear her phone ringing in the living room. She did a little sprint to find it and answer it before it stopped ringing. She had almost made it. She could see from the caller ID it was Dagan. More than likely, he had more questions to ask her about their conversation from the other night.

Tony was here working with Dagan on a case that supposedly had ties to that one and she found it to be very coincidental. She had read a small blurb on a news outlet on Facebook about the murders that had occurred in the Florida Keys that Tony had been involved in. The name of the person that was accused of the crime had stirred something in the far back reaches of her memory after they left, only she couldn't put a finger on it. It was familiar, but she couldn't recall why. She chalked it up to getting older and her memory not being what it used to be. Nothing in her life was like it used to be, and she feared that living alone was starting to take its toll on her. She would never tell Dagan that because he would insist on her living with him or some such garbage. She was too old and set in her ways to even consider something like that. Besides, she was praying that he and Dani would soon remarry and hopefully give her grandchildren. Her being there would interfere with the natural order of things and she was not going to be that type of mom.

She hesitated a brief moment before calling him back. The phone began ringing on the other end. It went straight to his voice mail. She left him a little message apologizing for missing his call and to call her back whenever he got a chance.

Chapter Nineteen

Information was finally starting to roll back into the coroner's office. Bill had already been on two phone conferences and three regular phone calls today, all pertaining to the seemingly endless number of remains he had from the asylum.

There had been quite a few people show up to the office claiming to have been related to someone that had once been a resident of the county wide infamous asylum. He had been rather surprised at the number of turnouts, he had thought there would be one or two maybe. He was glad for the help from the two assistants the state had sent him.

The results that were filtering back in was more than enough to keep him busy for the next few days. He could only imagine the anticipation these people had wondering if some of the remains that were no doubt being talked about in every coffee shop, café, and Wednesday night bible study group, were their long-lost relatives. Some were acting like there was some kind of lottery prize to be had, but he guessed fifteen minutes of fame was enough for these folks.

All the local newspapers in the areas had been running cover stories on it. Shelly had been fielding the phone calls from reporters and news stations wanting a statement from him. Thank God she had the common sense to tell them there would be no comments until the investigation was complete.

He picked up several of the reports shuffling through them trying to find the one that interested him the most. It was the one of the young girl that been a victim of coffin birth as well as whatever malady had put her in the ground to begin with. He found a separate note that was paperclipped to the report that had been written and specifically addressed to him by the state examiner.

It explained that when the state M.E. first heard there was a case of coffin birth that was being sent to the state lab, he had been very skeptical. Coffin birth was a rare occurrence mostly attributed to the medieval ages and those times before embalming was a popular practice. Given that this young girl would have died in a space of time going back to forty years or so, again approximately, he had assumed she would have been embalmed. Upon examination, he found the latter to be false. It was his assumption upon this fact alone she had been buried in a hurry. The only reason he had ever found to bury someone that quickly, outside the few religions that practiced it, would be to cover up something. As stated in his autopsy report, he found her death to be from homicide. Then he added the notation, for further facts, review the attached report.

Bill had come to the same conclusion during his exam, but because of the delicate nature of that particular set of remains, he had wanted confirmation. He read exactly what his own report had stated. He believed the victim to have died from a head trauma. There was a fracture in the skull that had been severe enough to cause death. He flipped through a couple of pages trying to find the DNA results. He was hoping that they had time to do those as well. But knew it could take forever sometimes for those to come back. Dagan had brought by a sample of DNA from a resident at a nursing home over in Marianna that could possible be the mother of the young girl in question. Bill had sent it off to be analyzed with the remains.

It was the very last page in the small stack of papers. He noted that she had lived in this general area all her life and had been well taken care of. There had been no signs of malnutrition. The report also concluded that the sample was a 99.9% match for maternity. They had indeed found the mother for this one unlucky girl. He would have to call Dagan and let him know so her mother could be notified. He jotted a note to himself on a note pad by his phone and went back to the report. It seemed that the state lab also run all the DNA samples though the national and federal DNA bases to see if any hits come back.

It seems that one had.

Not on the young girl, but on the baby. It was far enough along that there was a bit of DNA that could be extracted from the bones.

Bill removed his glasses and wiped his eyes, putting the glasses back on again. He could not believe who came back as a match for the paternity of this child.

Neither would Dagan and Tony.

Chapter Twenty

Dagan was glancing through the pictures that Mrs. Doyle had given him. He really saw nobody that stuck out to him at all. He barely recognized Donald Lockhart as a young man. The pictures he had seen of him were of an older man, who was quickly balding and slightly overweight. The younger version of him in these pictures looked like the boy in every family black and white photo from the years gone by you might see in your grandparents' house or in museums. His sister Andrea, AKA Alice, bore a resemblance to someone familiar but he couldn't seem to place her. There were lots of people related though in this neck of the woods, so it could be a distant relative of someone he had known along the way. She was striking with long black hair, and a waifish figure. It was a shame he couldn't have talked to her about her brother before she passed.

He would take these over to his mother later and let her look through them and see if she could recognize any of the faces or the names that Mrs. Doyle had written on the backs of each photo.

He found several messages on his desk and thumbed through them. The top one was from Bill's wife. She was giving him a retirement party in two weeks and wanted

Dagan, his mother, and Dani to attend. He called and spoke to her briefly letting her know that they would all three be there and asked her if it was alright to bring Tony along as well. She said of course it was ok. The more the merrier. He went to the next two messages, both from the farmer that claimed his cattle was being stolen. It seemed now he thought two of them had been brought back in the middle of the night. He was beginning to think this man was crazy, or else UFO and little green space men were real and had abducted them and then brought them back as soon as their experiments were through. More than likely they had wandered off into the woods and had now found their way back home. He shook his head. He really was looking forward the next election, so he could get back to his regular job. He was definitely not running for the office of sheriff.

The last message in his stack was from Bill stating that some of the results from the state were back and that he needed Dagan and Tony to come by to see him ASAP. He had imperative information on the case. That intrigued Dagan, so he walked out and threw the message down in front of Tony to let him read it for himself.

"What are we waiting for? Let's go." He said as he grabbed his hat off the chair that was sitting next to his desk.

They both were trying to make guesses at what Bill had found. They had no idea that the lid was about to be blown off the case, opening avenues that would give them a long over due break.

~ ~ ~

Bill had been expecting the pair, so he had told Shelly to send them back to the exam room. He had been working on a child that had a good possibility of being identified through the DNA results and the Isotope testing that he had requested. He was here comparing a few things when the two of them walked in.

"Hey coach. Whatcha' got for us?"

"Something you two are going to be glad to have, but not necessarily happy to hear about."

He walked over to a small table that had some books and papers on it and found a blue folder. He took one paper out and handed it to them. It seems the lady in the nursing home you interviewed the other day was a maternal match for our young mother. It is without a doubt her missing daughter, and grandchild. I'm not sure if she knew about the grandchild."

Dagan sighed. At least the lady could have some peace knowing that they had finally discovered what happened to her daughter, even if she was dead. He knew that feeling after finding his sister after she had missing for ten years. She too had been dead, but there was a sense of relief that she was no longer out there alone, and they could put her to rest at last. They would always know where she was now. He was sure that Mrs. Barnes would feel that same sense of relief.

"If she knew the girl was pregnant, she never mentioned it the other day." Tony said.

"Yeah, she told us her husband had their daughter placed there for being as she put it "flirtatious" and for sneaking out to the front porch one night to meet a boy. The records we found at the asylum had her labeled as an erotomaniac. I looked it up and found out it was just someone that believes others are in love with them. I guess you could call that a form of mental disorder, but not one that would require institutionalization in my book."

Bill just shook his head. "Other's were put there for a lot less."

Dagan and Tony shook their heads in sad agreement.

"That's not the only thing you two need to know. We were able to pull DNA from the baby, although it was just a small amount. It's amazing what they can do with that these days. They ran it through the federal and national databases and had a hit come back for the father."

Tony and Dagan looked at each other.

"But that would mean the father had been arrested or at the least had his DNA logged at one point for reasons other than wanting to know who his ancestors were." Tony offered.

"Oh, I'm quite sure after he died, they logged his DNA to make sure any crime that was found later on that had a possibility of being committed by him could be linked to him if necessary."

"Well, don't keep us waiting. Who is it?" Dagan asked anxiously.

"See for yourself." Bill handed him the folder.

Dagan looked at the paper on the top and couldn't believe what he was reading. "What the hell......." Then he grinned. He knew they had a solid lead now.

He pointed with his finger to the line that named the paternal match of the baby to show Tony just where to look.

The father was Donald Lockhart.

"You can't be serious? I mean, this is amazing. Things might start coming together now. We need to get back out there and talk to Mrs. Barnes and see if she recalls him ever coming around." Tony sounded excited.

"One more thing you two. Lyric Barnes was killed from a blow to the head. There is a fracture in her skull and both I and the state guy believe she was murdered. Now because she was more than likely buried quickly to cover her death up, that is why the coffin birth happened. That type of thing is a very rare occurrence." Bill explained.

"Well that would certainly fit. Of course, his MO was strangulation, but serial killers evolve and if she was his first kill, it might have been a different method." Tony told them. He had years of experience and knew that it wasn't unheard of for serial killers to start out with one method and changed to one that was more convenient.

"Thanks coach. We're going to head over there now to talk to her. Hopefully she can shed a little light on it for us."

The three said their goodbyes and Dagan and Tony hurried out to the truck. There was really no need to hurry, but they were both on fire with the news they had just received. The spoke of different scenarios that could have played out in the asylum all those years ago but the one that they agreed on and felt strongly was the most likely one was that when Donald was sent there as a youth, he had met Lyric and impregnated her. When he found out she was pregnant, he killed her. Given his thoughts on women, he had probably deemed her unfit as a partner and mother of his child because she had probably given in to him easily due to the condition she suffered from. Tony told Dagan that Donald had killed his own teenage daughter and her boyfriend because he had found out they two of them were going to have a child. If he would kill his own flesh and blood, there was no way he would have given a second thought to killing a girl who meant nothing to him but a few minutes of a good time.

They pulled into the parking lot and found a spot to pull the truck into. They entered the front door and noted there was no one at the reception desk, so they walked on back towards Mrs. Barnes room.

Her door was open, so Dagan knocked lightly and walked in after no one answered. The bed and chair by the window were both empty. The bed had been freshly made and the room smelled as if it was just mopped. Maybe someone had come to take her down to the recreation room where they showed movies, played bingo, and did other activities with the residents. As they were turning to walk out of the room, a nurse stepped in.

"Can I help you?" she asked.

"Yes ma'am. We're looking for Mrs. Barnes. We were here the other day and would like to see her again."

"Oh, I see. I'm sorry fellas but Mrs. Barnes passed away this morning. I guess you're a little too late." She said with empathy playing across her features. She looked as if she suddenly remembered something important. "Would one of you happen to be Sheriff Murphy?"

"Yes, that's me." Dagan answered.

"She was struggling yesterday and kept trying to tell us something. Of course, we couldn't understand her. She was incoherent. She did manage to find a piece of paper and pen and wrote this down and then addressed it to you." She handed Dagan the note and then left the room stating she had other things to attend to.

Dagan took the folded note that had sheriff written on it in a barely legible handwriting. He opened it and it just said the young man's name was Don. He showed it to Tony.

"Was she referring to the young man that had been caught with Lyric on the front porch, or the one she had met in the asylum?" Tony asked trying to connect the dots.

"And his name just happens to be Don? Short for Donald I'm presuming." Dagan answered.

"Our assumption was they met in the asylum."

"Maybe his arrest and subsequent trip to the asylum for being a peeping tom was all tied in to this incident. Lyric's father might have had him arrested to teach him a lesson and to keep him away from his daughter. Somehow, he ended up at the asylum, whether by his family's doing, or through the court system. Those records that would tell us how he got put there, are not among the ones we have looked though. I have been over them back and forth and sideways. Even the ones found at the asylum don't state who admitted him. That page was missing."

"I don't think the father had him put in the same place as his daughter. That would have been futile. We will probably never know the actual details because it seems everyone surrounding the mystery is dead. The theory works though so I say that is what we go on." Tony agreed.

They walked out of the dreary halls of the nursing home and into the bright sunshine. Dagan prayed he never had to live in a place like that and die all alone. He felt bad for Mrs. Barnes. She would never know that her daughter had been identified. She would never know that she might have been a grandmother if her daughter had lived.

He made himself and Mrs. Barnes a promise right then and there. They would be laid to rest side by side, and hopefully those three souls that had been torn from each other and the world were together at last.

Chapter Twenty-One

Dagan listened to his voice mail and heard his mother's message asking him to call her back. They were playing phone tag. He now had the box of photos to show her.

He returned her call, this time reaching her. They arranged to meet at the Blue Caboose for lunch, so he could show her the pictures and see if she recognized anyone in them.

In the meantime, he made some phone calls and found out through the nursing home that Mrs. Barnes had been catholic. He then called the catholic church to arrange to have a priest perform the funeral ceremony for Mrs. Barnes, her daughter, and grandchild.

The funeral home told him they had received payment for one casket and graveside services from a local church charity. Dagan was concerned about how he would be able to get another casket paid for, but the funeral director explained that it was indeed possible to have Lyric's and the baby's remains put in with the mother, although he would spare him the details on the process. Check that off his list. The funeral was set for two p.m. on Saturday at Tatter's Creek Cemetery. It had been named for the creek that ran through the back of the cemetery property and made for a serene setting.

He checked his watch. It was almost lunch, so he looked up through the window and saw that Tony was standing by the copier. He walked out and invited him to join him and his mom for lunch.

They arrived at the café and found a quiet table near the back. While they were waiting on Maureen, Dagan pulled out the pictures and made a neat little stack on the table. He had picked the ones with dates that would put his mom around the same age as the people in the pictures.

She arrived about fifteen minutes later just as the food he had ordered was delivered to the table. He had ordered his mom a Cuban sandwich, knowing that was her favorite. She sat down after hugging both "boys" as she still, and forever would, refer to them.

The first few minutes were filled with small talk and then she asked Dagan to get down to business. It made him laugh to hear his mom say that.

"Ok, mom, I was going to let you finish your lunch first, but if you insist." He handed her the stack of pictures. She looked at the top one and no recognition seemed to register. Dagan told her that there were names and dates on the backs of the pictures that might help.

She carefully perused each one, first looking at the photo, then flipping it over to read the information inscribed on the back. She had almost made it through the entire stack and Dagan was starting to feel defeated. She lingered on the last photo longer than she had the others. She flipped it over and read the names, then flipped it back over and gazed at it again. She seemed to be concentrating harder this time.

"Who is this girl Alice? Is she pertinent to your investigation?" she asked.

"Yes ma'am. Do you recognize her face or her name?" Dagan inquired with some hope.

"It says her last name is Dodd."

"It was. I told you about her when we came for dinner. She lived with her aunt and uncle until she found them murdered over in Bonifay. Her name was Andrea Lockhart, but when she moved in with her aunt and uncle they had her name legally changed her name to Alice Dodd."

She kept staring at the picture as if she was unable to look away.

"Mom, what is it?"

"Well, if I didn't know better...."

"Know what mom?" he asked impatiently.

"The dark hair isn't right. It's throwing me off. If the hair was blonde and cut in a short bobbed style, I could swear that this was Alice."

Tony looked confused. "It is Alice Mrs. Murphy. Alice Dodd."

"No. I mean Alice. Alice Taylor. My best friend, Dagan's godmother and former sheriff, his former boss." She looked up at Dagan in disbelief.

Dagan dropped the French fry he was about to put in his mouth and took the picture from her hand looking at it closely.

"The other night when you two came to dinner I thought hard about the name Lockhart. I never heard of them before. Then you mentioned the name Dodd. There was something about it, but I just couldn't place where I had heard it before. I thought it had sounded familiar because I probably heard it on the news or read about the murders in the newspapers. I wonder now if Alice ever mentioned it somehow in a passing conversation. She never spoke of her family. She had once told me that most of them were dead, and the others were not very nice people. She said she had cut all ties with them. I knew her as Alice Simpson, then Taylor. Those were her husbands' last names. "

"Are you sure about all this?"

"Look at that picture Dagan, you tell me."

He had felt a sense of familiarity when he had first seen it. Now it was as clear as day. Of course, he knew her as Alice Taylor, because that had been her married name, even though she divorced when he was small.

"I can say with certainty that's either her, or she had a twin. But even if she did have a twin, I don't think they would both be named Alice."

~ ~ ~

Dagan lay in his bed wishing Dani was beside him. Just her presence made him feel better. She had an apartment above the bookstore that she and Dagan split their time between and his house. She had been staying there so he and Tony could spend some time catching up.

So many things had spiraled and became tangled this past few weeks, and now it was all coming together. Alice, a friend of his family for years, had turned out to be one in the same as Alice Dodd, AKA Andrea Lockhart, sister to the serial killer Donald Lockhart.

He wondered if she ever knew what her brother had become. He was certain she had to. She was a sheriff after all and working in law enforcement. You couldn't get away from all the information that came across the wires and different venues. What if she knew and did nothing to try and stop it? Did she feel sympathy for him because of their childhood? Mrs. Doyle had said it had been rough for them both which is why Alice ended up leaving home in the first place. Or, was there a possibility that she actually didn't know he was anything other than what he chose to show the world?

Then you take the fact that they had found a massive burial site at the asylum and Donald just happened to be part of all of that too. He had once been a patient there and was father to an unborn child that had been found buried with its teenage mother, who was more than likely killed by him. Was she his first victim? They may never know. Thinking about all of this could drive a man insane.

He felt his eyes growing heavy as the moon began to rise higher in the sky. Soon enough it would start sinking lower and it would be time to get up and start all over again. Finally, his eyes closed, and his breathing evened out. Slumber had come, and he desperately needed the rest.

Chapter Twenty-Two

"For you were made from dust, and to dust you shall return. Amen."

The priest Dagan had contacted to perform the funeral rites for Mrs. Barnes and Lyric finished the ceremony with those few words. Dagan had ensured they had the proper ceremony with all the right things in place. It was the least this county could do for any of the victims of the asylum. The Methodist church had started a fundraiser so as each of the remains were identified, there would be money to give them a proper burial or cremation, no matter their denominational preferences. Dagan thought this to be one of the kindest things he had ever heard of.

There were only four people here today, besides the priest. Tony, Bill, himself, and Mrs. Doyle. When Dagan had told her about everything that had happened and what information he had on the members of her family, Donald and Alice, she felt it only right to be at the funeral. After all she told him, that baby would have been kin, a Lockhart. That poor little thing had been family. If there was one thing she had learned in all her years was family was family, no matter how good or bad they were.

She personally thanked the priest following the ceremony and placed a dozen white roses on the casket. Dagan had delicately explained to her that indeed, all three of them were in there, the funeral director had made sure that the three of them would be together for all eternity. She had found that heartwarming, since they had been ripped from each other in life.

He talked to Mrs. Doyle for a few minutes more promising her that he would soon return her photos to her along with any personal effects that had belonged to Alice they had packed up after her death. She told him she only wanted her photos. The things Alice left behind were of no use to her. Somehow, she felt they were tainted after she had heard about Donald, and what Alice had done in her own life. She felt that it had brought shame to her family and wanted nothing to do with any of them. She said her goodbyes and thank you to them all and headed back to her 1955 Ford pick-up. It wasn't in the best condition, but neither was she. It scared Dagan a little that the old lady was still driving. She threw her hand up to wave as she pulled off from the side of the road where she had parked, then took off in a cloud of dust.

Tony, Bill and Dagan had agreed they all needed a beer, or two. They would meet back at Bill's office to drink them. Because it was Saturday, nobody would be there working. Most of the remains had been autopsied and sent to state. There were a few that were being stored there, until the state could find the time to get to them.

They soon gathered in Bill's office and sat in the overstuffed leather chairs. Dagan wished he could say everything had been tied up in a perfect little bow, but there were still unanswered questions about the children who had suffered at the asylum. He supposed they would never know. Bill as much as told him sometimes it's best to let sleeping dog's lie. The past is the past, what's done is done, there's no going back and just about every other cliché the old man could think of. Dagan wasn't sure he would ever be the letting go type, but with no evidence at hand, he had no other choice. Nothing would ever change the way those kids had lived or died though.

He had heard the owners had decided to demolish it and start from the ground up and he had to agree that if anything was going to be built there, it should be brand new and not remnants of the past.

Bill popped the tops of three beers handing one to Dagan and Tony.

"Here's to my retirement and to never having to work a shit-storm case like this again." Bill held his bottle up and the other two men clinked bottles with his.

"I still can't believe the way it all turned out. To think Donald Lockhart was at the center of it all, not to mention our ex sheriff." Bill said taking a swig of beer.

"Yeah it's hard to wrap you mind around that's for sure." Tony added.

"I should have noticed something." Dagan said troubled.

Bill patted him on the shoulder. "Son, Sherlock Holmes would have had a hard time figuring out this mess. Don't beat yourself up over it."

"I'm trying not to. Alice just fooled everyone so easily. Especially my family"

"She was trying to hide her family's past and just happened to be very good at it." Tony chimed in. "She was in law enforcement long enough that she knew all the tricks. She had mad skills man. If I had to make a bet, I'd say she was the one who did away with some of the records and information we were looking for and had a hard time finding. I think she knew who and what her brother was and was trying to hide the fact she was related to him to protect her career. Who else would have left his record laying out like that at the asylum? She might have been going through them and something caused her to leave in a hurry."

"She was good at her job, I have to give her that." Dagan agreed. He thought back on the times he had been in the asylum and thought he had heard someone else in the building too. Could it have been her all along?

They made small talk through another beer and finally Bill announced, "Boys, I hate to break this up, but my wife is making my favorite supper tonight, catfish. I need to be on my way." He had grabbed his keys from his desk, so he could lock the front door as they walked out.

Tony and Dagan stood and told Bill they would see him at his party next weekend. They all agreed they were looking forward to it. Dagan told them it was nice to have something to look forward to for a change.

"Don't jinx it son, just be there."

"Come on coach, other than a serial killer who was born and raised here whose sister grew up to be sheriff and an old asylum with a bunch of dead bodies buried there, what could possibly go wrong?" He grinned at Bill.

Bill shook his head, made the sign of the cross and said flatly, "I'll see you boys next Saturday."

Chapter Twenty-Three

Bill sat in his favorite rocker on the wide front porch the south was so famous for. He stared out at the half mile long gravel road that led to the circle drive in front of the old farmhouse.

Soon there would be cars and trucks coming up the drive and parking wherever they could find a spot. His wife had planned a party to celebrate his retirement. He didn't want one, but her excitement had been infectious, so he let her have her way. He like to see her happy.

He reached over and turned the radio off. He had it out here, so he could listen to different ball games throughout the year, but right now one of those new so-called country singers was crooning about drinking tequila on a tailgate somewhere near a lake. That was what passed for country music today and it irritated him. Give him Merle Haggard, George Jones, and Loretta Lynn any day.

It was just a sign of the times he guessed.

He had seen a lot of change in his life. You don't live sixty-nine years and see the world stay the same. There were good times, not so good times, and some downright awful. That was the way of the world, bring you up, let you down and bring you back up again.

He was sure going to miss this place. It had been in the Walters family for the better part of one hundred and twenty years. His dad, grandfather, and great grandfather had all farmed it. At one time or another throughout the years the two hundred acres had yielded cotton, soy beans and peanuts. There had been smaller garden plots that his grandma and great grandma had taken care of with peas, beans, collards and such for the family's use.

He had been the odd ball that had never wanted to farm. He wanted to go to school. Of course, Viet Nam had derailed that for a while, but after he came home he went to medical school and the rest, as they say, is history. His dad had been disappointed at first, but eventually told Bill he was proud of him. That had been about thirty years ago right before he had passed away.

Bill had decided to sell the farm. He had no children to leave it to, and even if he had they probably wouldn't want it anyway. Young people today had no concept of the family homeplace and most didn't think it was important or care to keep the family history for future generations to learn from.

He had made a deal with All God's Creatures. They were a no-kill shelter for all kinds of animals including farm animals. He had asked for one stipulation. He wanted teachers to be able to bring their classes here on field trips to learn about different types of animals and how to care for them, how to take care of the land. Maybe that would give some hope to the future generations.

He got up and walked into the house letting the screen door slam behind him. He had done it since he was a kid, much to his mom and wife's irritation, and he didn't see the need to change it now. He saw his wife Betty and her two sisters running around carrying food trays to the back patio. He had offered to help earlier, but they had told him he would just be in the way.

~ ~ ~

That was his life now, old and in the way.

He waked out to the back patio that had been added in the late seventies when he and Betty had married and inherited the farm. It had been a necessity instead of a luxury. If there was one mosquito in a hundred-mile radius, it would find Betty. All other bugs seemed to have a thing for her too. He couldn't much blame them, he had a thing for the old gal himself.

When he walked outside, he saw his nephew laying out slabs of ribs on the huge grill that had been borrowed for the occasion. All this fuss made him shake his head, but he would smile and be gracious to make Betty happy.

He heard several cars doors slamming out front, so he walked around the corner of the house to greet the first guests that had arrived. It would be a steady stream now. So many faces from over the years, the span of three different careers. He had no idea how many people he had touched. It brought a tear to his eye. All this time he had thought of himself as grumpy, but these people had thought of him as a friend. Suddenly his mood lightened, and he was ready to have a good time.

~ ~ ~

The back yard was filled with dozens of people who had all had a part or a role to play in Bill's life at one time or another. His sister was here today with her two sons and husband. That was the only family he had left. He had a brother, but he had died from cancer when they were kids.

Betty was from a family of nine children, so most of the relatives here today were hers.

Looking around he realized that he had a good life. He counted himself lucky to have this many people that cared enough to be here today. Of course, there were a few he was sure might have come just for the free food. He smiled at his own surliness.

Dagan had seen him standing alone underneath the shade of an ancient pecan tree and headed in his direction.

"Nice party coach." He complimented.

"Yeah it is. Betty always did throw a mighty fine shindig."

"I think dang near everyone in the county is here today. You sure are popular. Not bad for a grumpy old man." Dagan teased.

"If there's anything I've learned in all my years on God's green earth is that people will come from miles around for two things. The first is a funeral, the other is a free meal."

Dagan laughed with his old coach. Betty joined them and slipped her arm around Bill's waist.

"Dagan, it's so good to see you. Is your mom and Dani here? There's so many people it's hard to tell."

"Yes ma'am. They are standing over there talking with that group of women." He said pointing in their direction.

"Well alright, I think I'll go on over and say hi." She gave Dagan a peck on the cheek and walked away. He blushed.

"You're a lucky man coach."

"That I am, son."

Tony had found them and wondered over to them and thanked Bill for including him in today's celebration. "I've never had BBQ that was this good."

"Eat all of it you want. Betty bought enough food to feed the entire panhandle. What doesn't get eaten today will be fed to me in ten different ways over the next week." The three of them shared another laugh.

Dagan spotted one of his deputies hurrying towards him with a frantic look on his face. What now, was his first thought.

"Sorry to interrupt sheriff. We have a situation out at Falling Waters State Park."

Falling Waters had long been a tourist attraction in Washington county. It was home to Florida's highest waterfall, which are a rarity in the state, and countless sinkholes that had boardwalks built over and around them for visitors to see.

"Exactly what kind of situation?" Dagan dreaded to ask.

"Two hikers just found a body. It looks like someone tried to throw it down one of the sinkholes."

"What the hell is going on in this county?" he asked to no one in particular.

"I don't have the details, they are just requesting you and Bill get out there pronto."

They all turned to look at Bill. He started shaking his head.

"No. Absolutely not. I retired. My last day was yesterday." He protested.

"But the new guy won't be here until Monday. We need an M.E, out there now." Dagan pleaded.

They all stood silent for several seconds.

"Dammit" Bill muttered as he walked off.

Dagan and Tony smiled at each other, but both felt sorry for the guy. It had to suck to leave your retirement party to go to work.

Bill pulled Betty to the side and explained to her what had happened. He apologized profusely to her. She patted his cheek and gave him a kiss.

He swore he would make it up to her. She swore she understood. She had always understood.

He joined Dagan, Tony and the deputy and together they all left the party to make the drive over to Falling Waters.

What a way to end a party and start retirement he thought, but he was who he was. A M.E., the county coroner. Whatever one might choose to call him. That was who he was today, until Monday morning rolled around, and the new guy showed up. Then everything would be different.

The scene they encountered at the park left them all reeling. None of them had ever seen what they were witnessing. They all prayed they would never witness it again.

Dagan knew that his small town was about to be terrorized.

Tony knew this was a lot bigger than a small-town murder based on cases he had already worked on.

Bill knew that his job would never really be over until the day he breathed his last.

All three felt a sharp sense of foreboding.

Evil had come to town.

= = =

The End
(Of the Florida Sheriff Deputies Series that is)
But, in the near future there will be a series of cases that Dagan and Tony will work together called *The Murphy and Giovanni Files*.
These stories will have graphic details of murders and victims. They will not be for the faint of heart.
Reader discretion is advised.

About the Author

After health issues caused Angela Jarvis to quit her job as a Physical Therapy Technician, she decided to devote more time to writing, which she has loved since her early teens. Angela lives in a very small town on the southern edge of Lake Okeechobee with her husband, daughter, and several fur babies. She has a grown son who is a sheriff deputy in the Florida Panhandle. He is a good source of information about law enforcement. "I find that ideas abound in a small town," says Angela. "Watching and listening is where all my best ideas come from."

Acknowledgments

As always, I thank God, for the abilities he has given me to tell the stories my mind creates.

For my family and friends who constantly ask me when the next book will be out and give big sighs when I say I'm almost finished, thanks for the impatience. It helps hurry me along!

To every single person who has bought my book, loaned it to other family and friends, and have recommended it, I thank you and hope you continue to enjoy my books.

www.angelakjarvis.com
angelakjarvis70@gmail.com

COMING SOON:

EVERGLADES INTRIGUE SERIES

As dark and mysterious as the Florida Everglades itself, comes this new series of modern-day murder and mystery mixed with the myths of yesterday.

The first book is set on the Seminole Indian Reservation involving their legend of the Ishtikini. A murderous owl creature of legend seems to be killing people, or is it a modern-day killer that is using that legend to cover up his crimes?

Read the next few pages for a special preview.

Shadow Of The Owl

Angela Jarvis

EVERGLADES INTRIGUE SERIES
(Book 1)

Let our last sleep be in the
graves of our native land.
- Chief Osceola

Prologue

The vast landscape of the Florida Everglades took on an entire other-world feel at night. Although it seems a magical place in the daytime, the darkness could bring about stirrings in the mind of ancient myths and legends. It was not a place to be out after sundown, if unfamiliar with the land. There were the animals that roamed around in the early evening looking for a meal, after the heat of the day kept them hidden deep in the swamp.

Dozens of species of plants and animals could be found here that nature lovers and photographers waded through treacherous terrain to find and take the perfect shot of. Hundreds of souls had been lost out here throughout history, never to be heard from or seen again.

There were the other things too. The things that came by night.

The things, that according to the elders, you were forbidden to speak of, lest you said the name aloud by mistake. To do so could call these things to you and bring your death. Only medicine men were allowed to speak the names of the forbidden, for they held the magic that kept them safe.

This is what Rose Tiger had on her mind as she paddled her way through the darkness towards a small, desolate island out in the middle of the Everglades. Thank goodness that the moon was bright and full tonight and gave her light to guide her along the way. The long dugout canoe glided silently cutting a smooth wake down a winding waterway, carved out by the Creator, who was grandfather of all things, long ago before man roamed the earth. One could get lost quickly if not careful of the surroundings.

Along with the normal sounds of the marsh at night of frogs, crickets, and pesky mosquitoes buzzing around her face, Rose heard a rustling above head close to the shoreline where she would have to land the canoe. To her right, on the branch of a dead cypress tree, sat a huge horned owl, his eyes glowing a golden amber in the moonlight.

He watched her curiously.

She kept her eye on him, but not because she was afraid he would attack her. She was thinking about the legend she had been told since childhood, and what him being here to greet her could mean. She shook her head and told herself to get a grip. Even though she had gone to the school on the reservation, so she could learn the Seminole language and customs, she had been to the white man's university. She now held a Bachelors degree and was a medical researcher for a new and upcoming pharmaceutical company. She did not believe in the old legends. He is only a huppa, which was the Seminole word for owl. Nothing more, nothing less, she told herself. A nocturnal creature that comes out at night looking for a nice fat mouse to eat.

She felt the tip of the canoe make contact with the shore and stepped out onto the muddy bank. Rose wanted to speak to the old woman who lived here alone in the middle of nowhere. She had tricked her cousin Marcus into telling her where the old woman's island was. He was a tour guide for the reservation and knew the back country so well, he could find these hidden places blindfolded.

There was an old footpath from the water's edge leading into a cypress head. She could

see an orange glow ahead.

Pushing the button on her flashlight and swatting at a gang of mosquitoes that just came out of nowhere, she was careful of her steps. She thought about the few details she could drag out of her grandmother earlier today as she walked.

Crazy Mary was once a powerful medicine woman for the tribe. According to Rose's grandmother, the woman's fiancé was killed in a tragic hunting accident, and she went crazy blaming the other three young men that had been with him that day. She cursed the others who

she felt responsible, and the village elders noticed her increasingly strange behavior over the next few months. Small animals were going missing, and she was blamed for doing evil rituals when some of their people became sick and their crops failed. She had refused the medicine that someone who had recently lost a loved one was supposed to take from the medicine man. The chief, along with a medicine man, went to her and told her she must leave the village and never return. She had been forced to live in isolation for the rest of her days, however long the Creator chose for that to be.

Rose was sure there was more to the story than what her grandmother had told her. She warned Rose not to speak of it again, but she needed to talk to the old woman. She had once possessed superb skills in the art of healing and knew all about the plants in the swamp that could be used to heal or harm.

The project Rose was working on could put an end to a terrible disease, the one that took her mother's life, and the old woman may hold that knowledge. Her grandmother told her the old woman was no longer human but filled with an ancient evil. She loved her grandmother dearly, but she just didn't believe in that nonsense. Crazy Mary was in her nineties according to her grandmother, so how much harm could she do anyone? Rose had tried searching the tribal records that were housed in the museum library, but it seemed that anything concerning her name had been purged.

She jumped as she heard the owl call out "who who... .who". He was now ahead of her down the path sitting on yet another cypress tree branch. She had not seen nor heard him fly by. That thing was really starting to creep her out.

The cypress head gave way to a small clearing, and in the middle stood a wooden shack on stilts. It was small and rundown. It seemed as if nobody lived there at all except for the small orange glow coming from one of the windows. Rose climbed a set of steps that led to the door and a small porch. She heard something land on the porch railing. The owl now rested there. The darn thing seemed to be following her.

Now, as the owl sat watching her, she moved carefully so as not to startle it. The moonlight caused him to cast an odd shaped shadow on the deck of the porch, but Rose kept her eyes focused straight ahead. Maybe if she ignored him, he would do the same for her. She knocked on the door and after waiting a couple of minutes, she knocked a little harder. Maybe the lady was hard of hearing, or maybe she just wasn't home. Where would she go out here at night?

Still no answer. She tried peaking in the window by the door, but it was covered in grime, so she could only see outlines in the mostly dark house.

She sighed out loud thinking she had come all this way at night for nothing. It was time to head back. She noticed the owl was gone now, and once again, she had not noticed him flying off nor had she heard him make any noise.

Walking down the steps she noticed a movement in the brush ahead of her. A blood curdling scream pierced the night and almost made her jump out of her skin. Calm down, she thought, it's probably a panther. She had heard their screams many times late at night. They could sound just like a woman screaming in pain. This was different though, it had a human quality to it. Not taking her eyes off the direction the screams had come from, she stepped down off the bottom step. The hair on her arms and the back of her neck stood up as if her body suddenly sensed danger. She was really starting to regret her decision to come out here and felt a twinge of guilt about not heeding her grandmother's warning.

Suddenly every sound in the swamp was quiet as if the air was sucked out of the clearing, and a woman stepped out of the woods. She was wearing the traditional long skirt of the Seminole women and a bright red shirt, with a belt that hung loosely about her hips. In her hand she carried a sack that was wet and dripping.

She didn't appear startled at all by Rose's presence. It was as if she had expected her. For a few moments they just stood and stared at each other before the old woman finally spoke.

"What are you doing here girl?" her voice had an ancient rasp to it.

"My name is Rose Tiger. I have come to speak to you. I wanted to ask you a few questions if you don't mind."

"I don't help anyone. Now leave."

"Please, if you'll only..." Rose was cut off.

"I said leave. You will find no answers here."

Rose thought about pleading her case more, but there was something in the old woman's eyes that told her it was futile. She had turned to walk away when the old woman spoke.

"You came out here be yourself?" the old woman asked, eyeing her curiously.

"Yes." Rose replied turning back around quickly.

"You're brave, I'll give you that."

The old woman started towards her. She noticed an odd smell but was unsure if it was the woman, or whatever was in the sack she was holding.

Rose took a step backwards asking, "May I come back some time to talk with you?

"You have free will to do whatever you want, but I am not responsible for anything that might happen to you while you are here." Her gait was slow, but she held herself upright and as proud as someone half her age.

As the old woman passed by her, Rose felt a sense of relief. She had to admit the tales she had heard earlier had her wondering if the old woman truly had special powers. She glanced down at the sack the old woman held in her hand.

She finally realized the smell she had noticed earlier was the smell of copper. Rose stifled the impulse to scream.

The sack the old woman carried was soaked with blood.

TO BE CONTINUED ...

For sales, editorial information, subsidiary rights information
or a catalog, please write or phone or e-mail
AbsolutelyAmazingEbooks
Manhanset House
Shelter Island Hts., New York 11965, US
Tel: 212-427-7139
www.BrickTowerPress.com
bricktower@aol.com
www.IngramContent.com

For sales in the UK and Europe please contact our distributor,
Gazelle Book Services
White Cross Mills
Lancaster, LA1 4XS, UK
Tel: (01524) 68765 Fax: (01524) 63232
email: jacky@gazellebooks.co.uk